RESISTING
the Bad Boy

BOOK ONE

VIOLET DUKE

THE *can't resist* SERIES

Copyedits and Proofreading by Victory Editing, Danielle Romero, and Margaret Rainforth

ISBN: 1941198015
ISBN-13: 978-1-941198-01-8

Printed in the United States of America

10 9 8 7 6 5 4 3 2

OTHER BOOKS BY VIOLET DUKE

The CAN'T RESIST Series
RESISTING THE BAD BOY *
FALLING FOR THE GOOD GUY *
CHOOSING THE RIGHT MAN *
FINDING THE RIGHT GIRL
KEEPING THE REBOUND FLING *(Winter 2015)*
HAVING THE REAL THING *(Spring 2016)*
Three-Book serial trilogy, also available in the NICE GIRL box set

The CACTUS CREEK Series
LOVE, CHOCOLATE, AND BEER
LOVE, DIAMONDS, AND SPADES *(*New* Added to series 2/15)*
LOVE, TUSSLES, AND TAKEDOWNS
LOVE, EXES, AND OHS *(Spring 2015)*
LOVE, SIDELINES, AND ENDZONES *(Spring 2015)*
LOVE, STILETTOS, AND CUFFLINKS *(Fall 2016)*
LOVE, MEDDLING, AND MISTLETOE *(Fall 2016)*

The UNFINISHED LOVE Series *(Cactus Creek Reunions)*
Book 1 & 2: Caine & Addison *(Summer 2015)*
Book 3 & 4: Gabe & Hannah *(Summer 2015)*
Book 5 & 6: Max & Kennedy *(Fall 2015)*
Book 7 & 8: Drew & Skylar *(Winter 2015)*

-- *Coming in 2016 from Penguin Random House* --

The FOURTH DOWN Series *(Cactus Creek Nights)*
Book 1: (Jackson's story) Title TBA
Book 2: (Bennett's story) Title TBA
Book 3: (Donovan's story) Title TBA

DEDICATION

To my wonderful husband and two amazing kids.

BOOK DESCRIPTION

The book that started it all. Book One of the Nice Girl trilogy, the acclaimed three-book serial that began the New York Times, USA Today, and worldwide bestselling CAN'T RESIST series.

Abby Bartlett is the quintessential nice girl. Between teaching, volunteering, completing her PhD, and helping her best friend raise his daughter, Abby never gets the chance to be anything but nice. That is, until the all-wrong-for-her man she's only ever known from afar starts daring her to simply take that chance for herself. His sage advice?

Try something wild and fast.

Preferably him.

An unbridled, hotshot attorney with a not-so-little black book, Connor Sullivan has earned himself quite the bad boy reputation. But in his defense, he's a very conscientious one. He knows far too well that sometimes in life, love isn't enough...or worse, not even a factor at all. To avoid that misery—and repel the drama—Connor always makes his one and only rule crystal clear right from the start.

Absolutely nothing more than a month.

Turns out, a whole lot can happen in one month.

CHAPTER ONE

GLANCING ACROSS THE ROOM at his guests, Connor Sullivan was pleasantly shocked to see his brother Brian arrive at the party with a date on his arm.

As most everyone in his house tonight could attest, Connor wasn't used to failing. He was one of the most sought-after corporate attorneys in the Western U.S. with a courtroom reputation even his friends referred to as notorious—due in part to the impressive number of times and ways he's been held in contempt for his clients.

So sue him, he enjoyed the rough and tumble victories. He fought hard for his wins, and he did it well.

But when it came to helping his little brother cope with being a widower at the age of thirty, Connor had no clue who to fight, or how to win.

Aside from paying off a decade's worth of hospital and care facility bills from his sister-in-law's battle with early-onset Huntington's, and creating a scholarship in Beth's name for youth plagued with the debilitating disease, Connor had felt useless to Brian after her death. All he'd been able to do was give him space, the only thing Brian insisted he needed.

For nearly a year.

Logically understanding that Brian had to tackle this on his own didn't make it any less of a bitch for Connor; it just made him craftier about how he snuck in the big brother thing.

Luckily, it was summer in Arizona, he had a pool, and Brian had a pre-teen daughter. Simple as that. After a month of regular family cookouts, it was no longer uncommon for Brian to show up at the house unannounced, grab an unoffered beer, and plant himself on the couch to catch a game uninvited.

It was nice having his brother back.

For the better part of a decade, Brian's singular mission had been to give his wife a lifetime's worth of happiness every day, while hiding his own anguish over her heartwrenching physical and psychological decline. Connor knew it used to kill Brian to watch Beth gradually give up raising her own child the worse her motor functions became. Even *before* she'd become bedridden.

That's when Connor had begun jumping in to watch his niece Skylar as much he could, mainly since the eldest Sullivan matriarch had about as much experience being a warm grandma as she'd had being 'mom' instead of 'mother' when he and Brian were kids.

In fact, she'd specifically *asked* to be third in the caretaker line-up—meaning in dire asteroids-falling-from-the-sky cases only—following Brian's friend from college, a nice girl Connor vaguely recalled meeting years ago.

Between the two of them, they were never in the same place at the same time, but somehow managed to take the place of one full-time secondary caretaker whose sole mission was to shield Skylar from what was happening to her mom.

There had been no shielding Brian, however.

Truth be told, while Connor had always admired Brian's extraordinary, wholly nonhereditary capacity for love, he'd been a little glad to see the tragic love story finally come to an end.

Awful as that sounds.

He'd adored his sister-in-law, really. But the time was long past for Brian to move on with his life.

Tonight, it looked like he was finally starting to.

"I'm going over to say hi to my brother. Do you want to come along or are you good here?" Connor asked his date for the night, the always stunning Victoria, a divorce lawyer from a rival firm who just happened to be between men this week.

"Brian's here tonight? How wonderful," replied Victoria with her token radiant smile, the most effective tool in her arsenal to detract attention from her constantly wandering eyes. "Give him my best will you? I'm going to mingle. The Adonis in the gray pinstripe is looking mighty lonely there in the corner."

Connor rolled his eyes. "Alright, have fun. Just be sure to stay away from the men at my firm…the women too, for that matter. Last year alone, you sent our sweet, bright-eyed bankruptcy fifth-year into a funk and later had two of the probate guys ready to kill each other."

He frowned in remembrance of that catastrophe. "Actually, you know what? Check where they work before you even start speaking to them at all."

"No promises," she sang out as she sashayed off.

He sighed. Despite the very real threat her refusal to behave was sure to present, Connor still found himself smiling after her. Victoria was the only constant female in his life for four years running now. How that managed to happen was one of life's great mysteries. He supposed she fell in the friends with benefits category, though calling her a friend was a bit of a stretch…and he'd politely stopped all transactional 'benefits' after the first month.

Okay, so she was more of a trophy-date-on-demand with a well-advertised rolling re-enrollment policy on lapsed benefits.

That aside, they actually had a very nice thing going. She'd accompany him to black tie functions to save him from vapid socialites on the prowl, and he'd reciprocate if ever she needed.

Fortunately, her revolving dating door spun faster than his did so he rarely had to carry out his end. Not that she wasn't a nice enough woman. But her glib old money view on the world was a bit much to take at times.

Hearing the unmistakable peal of Victoria's flirt-giggle carry across the room, Connor found himself mildly curious about who she was trying to close, so soon in the game. Peering over, he snorted out a laugh when he saw it was none other than Clay Gibbs, the man who put the ass in pompous.

The only reason Connor let his assistant invite the privileged nitwit tonight was because Clay was a third generation firm client on a very short leash. With him here, the bail money they kept in the safe for him actually had a fighting chance to remain there.

"Oh, what a surprise, Victoria didn't stay to say hi."

The long lost sound of Brian busting his chops had Connor beaming ear to ear—it'd been a while since he'd heard him do it. "Yeah, well, you know Victoria."

"Nope, I sure as hell don't. And I prefer to keep it that way."

Connor chuckled. "I'll be sure to tell her there's a man in Arizona inexplicably immune to her charms. Glad you could make it out tonight, man. And with a lovely date, no less."

Looking over at the pretty brunette standing beside Brian, Connor had to work hard to keep his reaction in check. Seeing her vintage pin-up girl figure from across the room earlier, he hadn't expected the face accompanying the voluptuous body to be so…sweet.

Wholesome even.

"I'm Connor," he said smiling, thrown a bit by the quick glimmer of humor he saw flash in her eyes.

"Hi, Connor. It's nice to see you again."

Again? Crap, did he know her?

He carefully scanned her fresh-faced features once more. Wide, guileless eyes—a charming novelty he was positive he hadn't encountered in years—untinted lips, a light tan that actually appeared to be from the sun, and deep, dark reddish brown locks done up in a ponytail more comfortable than fashionable.

There was no way in hell he knew her.

She was the very definition of a buxom beach babe brunette, if such a category existed, with an appealing blend of innocence and intelligence behind a pair of unaccountably sexy, cliché-free glasses. Definitely not his usual type.

Pity.

"I'm so sorry, have we met before?"

Brian glared at him, looking more than a little disappointed. "Dude, it's Abby. Abby Bartlett?"

This was Brian's friend from college? Wow, she sure grew up. In a nice girl with a hot halo sort of way.

"Abby, of course. My apologies. We met in the hospital right after Skylar's birth."

Those deep brown eyes of hers were outright

laughing at him now. "And maybe a couple more times since then."

Well that just ratcheted his chagrin up to full-blown guilt.

Her quick hey-don't-sweat-it smile didn't help one bit...the playful brow tilt that followed soon after, however, did. "Relax, Connor. How about this—the next time you introduce yourself to me again, I'll be sure to pretend I know what the inside of your house looks like for 'other' reasons. Be all indignant. Make you squirm a bit. That ought to square us."

Surprised laughter built in his chest. How about that? Talk about intriguing. Before he could banter right back, however, a nearby voice broke into their conversation, "Professor Bartlett, is that you?"

Professor?

Spicy upgrade from cute librarian. Connor was hooked.

The line and sinker came when he then proceeded to witness Abby scold—actually scold—his firm's best civil litigator.

"How many times do I have to tell you to cut that out? My PhD is *not* a done deal, Jim."

"Oh hush, young lady." James T. Holt came over to give Abby a formal peck on the cheek. "As far as I'm concerned, 'ABD' stands for all but done. You may as well get used to being called a professor." Jim turned to bring Connor up to speed. "I've known Abby here for years.

She's a miracle worker. Thanks to her, my son was actually able to move on to high school this year."

"Reese was *not* that bad," defended Abby, hands on hips.

"Says the woman who only had him in small doses," replied Jim dryly. "I'm just glad you started tutoring at his school when you did. I was really starting to get worried."

"That you'd have to dust off the ole grammar knowledge you 'misplaced' to attempt to help him with his homework?" ribbed Abby.

Connor blinked. Seriously, who was this woman?

Jim chortled heartily. "You caught me. Thank God for well-written paralegals and first-years."

"Hence my stand on standardizing a more rigorous business and technical writing curriculum in core education."

Abby threw an I-told-you-so grin over at Brian. "Brian, this is James Holt, one of the greatest legal minds in the city...well, next to your father and brother of course. James, this is Brian Sullivan of *those* Sullivans," she editorialized behind an impishly cupped hand. "He's the rebel son who chose the career path of teaching business economics over lawyering."

Brian and Jim shook hands and immediately launched into conversation over current commerce affairs.

Never had Connor felt so invisible.

"You can get back to your party now," said Abby in a conspiratorial tone. "No worries, I'll keep an eye on

Brian for you tonight."

The innocuous words hit him like a bucket of ice on his lap, shriveling his growing interest in the woman right up. Reality check, jackass—she was *Brian's* date.

Brian's smart, captivating, completely off-limits date.

He took a blatant step away from the all too fascinating Abby and fumbled for a recovery, "I, uh…thanks. For taking care of it for me. Him, not it…Brian, that is."

Rendered idiotic by the amused, utterly female smile curving her plump lips, he finished lamely, "You're good for him."

"Thanks, Connor." She grinned. "I've always thought the same of you."

Lord, he could listen to the way she said his name all day, her husky teacher voice an inspiration for instant fantasies of the lusty sex-in-the-classroom variety.

Yep, he had to get the hell away from her. Fast.

"You're right, I should return to my guests. It's been a pleasure, Abby. Enjoy your evening." With that and a cursory nod, he excused himself like a bat out of hell, waiting until he was safely at the other end of the room before allowing himself one final glance back.

Just in time to see Brian whispering in her ear, of course.

CHAPTER TWO

"YOU WERE GETTING READY to hit on Victoria."

"What?! *No!*"

Abby snickered at the degree of horror in Brian's voice as she recounted the party events from two nights prior. "Yup. It was a close call, too. I got you out of your brother's house when you started saying how hot she was." She tsked into the phone. "I told you all that expensive liquor Connor keeps would sneak up on you harder than the cheap stuff we drink."

"Still. *Victoria?*"

She could almost hear him shuddering.

"Good god, I'm glad you saved me when you did. I knew it'd be a good idea to bring you to that party."

"Except now Connor thinks you and I are dating."

"So what if he does?" queried Brian indifferently. "Maybe now he'll stop giving me those pitying looks he thinks I don't see. You don't mind playing along, do you?"

She thought about it for a second. "No, I guess not. I only see the man every few years or so."

And he evidently only remembers me every ten.

The pity party from that depressing fact was quickly broken up by the blaring school bell over the phone line. She checked the time. "Is that the end of lunch for you?"

"Yeah, but I have a prep period next."

"Nice. So, how's the first day going so far?"

"Great if you don't count how many rabid alpha students I have again this year," he grumbled, though affectionately. "I swear, some of these kids think they're getting their MBAs. If their term projects weren't *coincidentally* due right before winter ball and prom, I'm pretty sure they'd turn in fifty-page papers."

Coincidence. Sure.

If she had a penny for every time she'd had to help him grade papers at the last minute, she'd be loaded. Though a brilliant teacher, Brian had astonishingly little regard for assessments.

"Oh hey, speaking of school dances," Abby grinned finkishly, "I hear Skylar can look forward to her first one in the spring. You freaking out yet?"

Brian groaned. "Don't remind me. My blood pressure is not ready for a preteen daughter going to a dance with boys. Did she call you specifically to complain about my lack of joy in all this?"

"Actually she told me when I was over there yesterday."

"You came over?"

"During the four hours you slept off your hangover, yes."

"Ah, that solves the case of the missing dirty dishes."

"Guilty. Oh, and I tasted the culinary genius you made her before you went back to bed by the way. I thought the Cajun flavored eggs had a superb crunch."

"Why, thanks. Charred shell bits give it an extra zing, I think."

"Not to mention added protein, too…which went well with the waffles I made her."

He sighed. "Have I mentioned how much I love you?"

"Often. Why just the other night, I recall at least a dozen instances. The fact that they were all localized to my chest area as I dragged your drunk butt into your house didn't diminish the heartfelt sentiment behind the words one bit."

"*Shit.*" The horror returned to his voice. "Okay, that's it, no more of the devil's juice for me. I clearly can't handle the stuff."

She gasped in mock alarm. "You mean our MMA fight nights will be limited to pizza and *soda*?"

He paused. "Good point. I guess I'll have to keep beer on the list of acceptable beverages. Just for you."

"Aw, you're so good to me," she chuckled as she checked the time again. "Shoot, I better get going. I'm meeting with a few teachers about expanding my tutoring roster this year."

"I thought you weren't going to start volunteering until September," he admonished sternly. "Abby, you can't keep putting off your dissertation. Those kids can get by without you."

"Just setting things up, I promise. Fear not, I'm sticking to my plan. Just me and my laptop 'til I go back to work next month."

"Good. I already instructed Skylar to gather her friends and chase you out of school if you show up over the next three weeks. We also blacked out every day on the calendar until ASU is back in session to remind us to leave you alone."

"No need to go that far. I won't be writing the entire time. And since my teaching line is straight freshman comp again this semester, I'm all set with my syllabus and lesson plans already. I'm sure I'll have pockets of time to hang out here and there."

"Well, then you can go get reacquainted with your colleagues and the other equally brainy candidates in your program. Go get all academic again. Skylar and I have been monopolizing your time way too much lately. If you're not careful, you'll find yourself in front of your doctoral defense panel dropping Skylar's OMGs and my far more delightful f-bombs."

Oy, her professors would think she was having a seizure and send her back to pre-dissertation comp exams for sure.

"Besides," he continued, "we've already begun the detox process to do without our Abby fix for a few weeks. Sure, we'll be strung out since you've gotten us all addicted to your greatness, but we'll be fine," he assured softly. "Really."

A wash of tears stung her eyes. "Okay. Well you tell Skylar I'm never too busy for her. Or her dad."

"Sure thing." The awkward pause that followed had him quickly clearing his throat. "Alright, my prep period's almost up so I better finish eating. Happy writing, babe."

Abby hung up the phone with a pinch of sadness. Three whole weeks without talking to Brian on a daily basis?

Huh.

Ten-to-one odds he'll crack first.

———◆———

ABBY EYED THE OMINOUS black clouds that had appeared out of nowhere sometime during her last meeting of the day.

"Great," she muttered, rubbing her bare arms. Arizona's unpredictable monsoon season at its finest.

In a mocking curtsy, Mother Nature smoothly edged out the last tiny bit of blue in the sky and dumped a city-dousing waterfall of rain onto the ground within a six-second window.

Lovely. Not even a nice drizzle to give her a head start. At least she had on sneakers today.

"*Don't you even think about it!*"

Abby spun around to see Evelyn Ramirez, the English department head, running down the hall with a fire hydrant yellow *Piñon Pine Middle School* rain cloak. "You were going to run out in that downpour, weren't you?" she accused as she slapped the school spirit poncho into Abby's grateful hands.

Abby smiled sheepishly. "I don't live that far away."

A disapproving headshake was all she got back as she donned the thin plastic, glad that it was long enough to cover the book bag at her hip. "Thanks Eve. I'll return it tomorrow."

"You most certainly will not. You're not coming in, remember? That dissertation isn't going to write itself, missy. And if you come around after school one day with your big bleeding heart, these kids will pounce and *suck you dry.*"

At Eve's fierce look, which was at least half serious, Abby laughed. "Okay, I'll keep it as a reminder of just that."

A crash of thunder made them both jump. Eve studied the courtyard through the sheets of rain coming down. "That's a storm, alright. You better just make a break for it now."

Abby was thinking the same thing. After a final thanks, she darted out into the pounding rain.

Exiting the school premises, she cut to the shortest route back to her house, resigned to splash through ankle-deep road puddles to save time. With just under a block left to go, however, she slowed down when she spotted a girl huddling under an anorexic sidewalk tree, trying in vain to stay dry.

"Skylar?" she called out, wiping the water out of her eyes to make sure she was seeing correctly.

The girl's guarded stranger-danger expression dissolved into a relieved smile. "Abby, hi!"

Running over, Abby again cursed the fickle Arizona weather when she saw that Skylar was similarly not dressed for the rain. "Why aren't you at your Uncle Connor's? You promised your dad you'd walk straight over there right after school."

"I stayed back after school for a little bit to sign up for some clubs. But then out of the blue, it started pouring like crazy. I've been trying to call my dad because I figured he and Coach Bill canceled fall football tryouts today but he isn't answering his cell."

"Your dad had a faculty meeting before practice today so he probably doesn't have his phone on." Without thinking twice, Abby immediately yanked off her new sunbright rain barrier and slipped it over Skylar's head.

"What are you doing?"

"I have way more padding than you, hon. You need

this more than I do to stay warm." While Skylar was busy trying to find the poncho's elusive armholes, Abby rustled around in her bag for one of the plastic bags she usually kept in case she needed to carry library books when she was doing research.

Finally fnding one, she wrapped up her book bag to protect it from the rain. "Okay, there are no two ways about it, we just have to make a mad dash for your uncle's house." She gripped Skylar's hand. "Ready?"

Skylar's wary '*not really*' was still hanging in the air under the tree when Abby yanked her out into the rain and started them on a frantic six-block sprint uphill in the opposite direction of her own home.

By the time they got to Connor's mini McMansion, Abby was sure she looked like a drowned stray cat. She certainly felt like one.

Racing up his absurdly long driveway, she wordlessly pointed to the side yard, knowing she'd never be heard over the drumming rain. Skylar just nodded and followed her around the house to the back porch. The night of the party, Abby remembered seeing a mudroom of sorts at that entrance. As waterlogged as they were, she didn't want to go near the grand front entry.

"OMG! That was insane!" screeched Skylar when they finally managed to dive under cover.

Chortling in agreement, Abby clutched her side and tried to catch her breath.

A long distance sprinter she was not.

As soon as she was physically able to speak without gasping, she pushed Skylar into the house. "Go in and get warmed up. I'm sure your uncle has an old t-shirt and drawstring swim trunks you can borrow while you throw your wet clothes in the dryer. If he doesn't, or if they look to be made out of some fancy materials worth more than your iPod, text me and I'll drive back over here with some spare clothes."

"Wait, you're going? You can't walk back to your house in all this rain. Come in and wait it out."

Abby shook her head. "I don't think it's going to let up, kiddo. I'll be fine. A few more minutes of rain won't kill me."

"Well at least let me find you an umbrella. I'll go check the closets." Skylar bounded down the hall, clearly knowing where she was going in this museum of a home.

"Don't track water onto the carpet!" Abby hollered after her, marveling over the echo that bounced off the crown molding and pristine marble floors.

Why a hardcore bachelor like Connor needed such a huge, extravagant house was beyond her.

Realizing that she was dripping all over the nice flagstone porch, she went over to the covered walkway near the garage to wring out about a gallon of desert rain from her hair.

Normally, she loved having long, thick hair that could knock out an innocent bystander if she attempted to do a shampoo commercial hair flip.

Today was not one of those days.

Bent over and focused entirely on squeeze-drying the wet blanket of hair cloaking her face, Abby almost toppled onto her head when a voice sounded out from above, *"What are YOU doing here?"*

Abby shut her eyes and shivered.

Not because she was soaked and freezing her ass off. But because she was suddenly hot. Very hot. Tear-your-clothes-off broiling. And the dangerous spike in her temperature had everything to do with that low, raspy growl.

Or rather, the man behind the growl.

Connor.

She dragged in a slow breath and let the heat of his deep voice warm her like a luxurious fire for a beat…until it occurred to her—a few brain-foggy seconds later—that his clipped question earlier had been absolutely dripping with disdain.

Startled, she looked up to confirm her suspicions.

Sure enough, Connor was standing there positively glaring at her, his lips curled in a contemptuous sneer, well into the territory of hostile.

"Don't worry, *Abby*, I'm not going to introduce myself to you again today." He eyed her up and down. "So what's the story behind all this? Did you somehow get lost on the way to Brian's? Or did you perhaps follow the yellow brick road here thinking it was paved with gold?"

Her jaw dropped. "Ex*cuse* me?"

"Honestly, after how Brian's gone on and on about you over the years, I never figured you for a brother-hopper. I can't believe you'd do this to him. What was the big plan? Sneak back onto my property and attempt to seduce me in that trampy get-up?"

His eyes dropped mockingly to her drenched chest, which was basically naked under the now transparent fabric plastered to her body like shrink-wrap. "Did you really think *that* was going to tempt me enough that I'd forget you're dating my brother?"

He scoffed coldly and drilled her with a glower. "Let's face it, honey, you're not exactly the wet t-shirt type."

Trembling with an equal amount of outrage and hurt, Abby shot him with the most lethal look she could muster before scrambling back to the porch and grabbing her book bag on the fly.

Without another word—though she had a few choice ones in mind—she turned and took off down the driveway.

Away from that colossal asshole.

CHAPTER THREE

As CONNOR WATCHED ABBY flee his lot, upset and clearly mortified, he wondered why the sight of her tears was having such an effect on him.

It's not as if she were the first woman he'd shot down for showing up at his house half-dressed and looking for a good time. She was, however, the only one he'd ever had to turn away because of his brother.

Okay, so a part of him felt like a jerk for what he'd said to her. But just picturing how bummed Brian would be about all this was enough to send those guilty feelings packing.

Running off with her tail between her legs was the very least she deserved for screwing with Brian. Connor just hoped his brother wasn't too serious about her yet.

The fact that the two had been best friends for so long surely complicated things.

Regardless, he'd be brutally honest and help Brian nip the doomed relationship in the bud before she broke his heart down the line.

There would be no backseat-brothering on this one.

Standing idly by while Brian had limited his life to just plain existing for the past year had been torture.

But it had been a cakewalk compared to seeing him spend a decade waiting for a horrible illness to slowly kill the love of his life.

Beth had been Brian's world, his high school sweetheart, the girl he'd come home vowing he was going to spend his life with the day he'd met her.

Receiving the devastating news that Beth's time with him would be far shorter and infinitely rougher—mere weeks after their unplanned child was born—simply prompted Brian to love and live every day following like it was their last.

And he'd only been nineteen at the time.

Connor wouldn't wish that on his worst enemy.

Day after day, he'd watched Brian go to that hospital room and whisper reminders to Beth of how much she was loved, long after the dementia from her disease had stolen everything that was sweet and good in her...along with all her memories of her husband and child.

Honestly, Connor wasn't sure he'd have been able to survive it had the roles been reversed, and God knew the years before the hospitalization had been just as bad, in an entirely different way. He still got chills thinking of the day he'd heard Beth's slurred voice screaming for Brian to take Skylar and leave, let her kill herself to end it all.

Damn that disease.

"Uncle Connor? What are you doing home?"

Connor almost jumped out of his skin.

Shit, *Skylar*.

The whole reason he was home this afternoon to begin with.

It was no secret Connor adored his niece Skylar. And with him living so close to the middle school she'd just gotten a boundary exemption to attend, her walking over to his home while he was at work had been his no-brainer solution to Brian's dilemma over whether to go back to coaching afterschool this year.

Fast forward to today, however, and Connor had found himself envisioning everything from kidnappers to sudden black holes opening up in his quiet street for most of the morning.

It was just a few measly blocks for crying out loud but he couldn't help it. After the rough hand the universe has dealt the poor girl, they were all a little overprotective of her.

Hell, Brian had moved mountains just to get Skylar into this new school to begin with. The minute he'd found out that Skylar's best friend would be moving away not long after Beth's passing, Brian had begun a campaign involving everything short of stalking the educational board to get district approval so the two best-friends-since-daycare could at least be in the same school again this upcoming year.

Thank God it had worked out.

Connor couldn't imagine what it was like for an eleven-year old to lose her mom the way she did. She'd barely said one word throughout the entire holiday season last winter. Really, the school transfer was the first thing she'd seemed truly happy about all year.

Ditto for her dad.

And now this Abby fiasco to add to everything Brian's already been through? For Pete's sake, couldn't the universe give his little brother a break for a change?

His silent Abby-riled diatribe temporarily forgotten at the sound of Skylar coming up beside him on the walkway, Connor immediately shifted to damage control assessment.

What were the chances that Skylar had caught the full frontal of Abby all slutted-up just now?

With Abby being the closest thing Skylar had for an aunt, how the hell was he supposed to explain this without traumatizing the poor girl?

Damn that woman for putting me in this situation.

"Why hello to you too, princess," he tossed out casually, turning to greet her with a smile. "I had a few hours free so I thought I'd hang out with you on your first day here."

"Oh, cool." She looked around. "Hey, where'd Abby go?"

Fan-frickin-tastic. "So you saw her here, huh? She wasn't here long…she just stopped by to, uh—"

"She *left*?" A too-mature frown marred Skylar's little pixie face. "I told her to wait 'til I brought back an umbrella for her." Shaking out a butt-ugly yellow rain slicker, she pouted some more. "And she didn't even take back her poncho!"

He did a double take. "What do you mean?"

"Abby lent it to me before we ran over here."

Gulping, Connor felt cold hard shame start to prickle over his skin. "Abby ran all the way here in the rain with you?"

"Yeah, it started coming down right when I left school. She found me under a tree trying to stay dry."

Skylar surveyed the rapidly worsening weather worriedly. "Dad will totally kill me if she catches a cold this week with all her…*wait a sec*—" She swung a suspicious look back his way. "Abby never leaves without saying bye. Did you say something to her?"

Smart girl.

Choosing to sidestep her question for the time being, Connor pulled out his smartphone and asked instead, "Do you spell Abby's last name with two T's or one at the end?"

"Two." She raised a brow. "Why? Are you looking her up to *apologize* for something? If so, I have her cell phone number."

He sighed. "Unfortunately, I don't think a simple apology is going to cut it. I think I need to send her a whole bunch of sorry-I-was-such-an-idiot flowers."

"Holy moly, what did you say to her?"

He again, refrained from answering.

No need to piss his niece off too.

Quickly texting a request for his assistant to order him the most extravagant floral arrangement she could find, he ignored his niece's interrogation once again. "You wouldn't happen to know Abby's address would you?"

"Nope." A slow, serves-you-right smile hooked her lips. "But dad does."

Silently, he unleashed a string of expletives and began estimating what the going rate was for bribing a kid nowadays.

It'd be worth it for the stay of execution by Brian's hand.

———•———

"HOW THE HELL did you find out where I live?"

Connor winced, but stood his ground atop Abby's doorstep. Thankfully, the gigantic doorway-filling flower arrangement his assistant had purchased for him was allowing him to hide for a few precious seconds longer.

Blindly shoving the flowers forward, he waited for Abby to take them.

When she didn't, he took a peek around the massive bouquet to see if she was even still there. She was.

And she was trying her damndest not to laugh.

"Is this monstrosity for a funeral?"

Grateful for the buried humor he heard in her voice, he let out the breath he'd been holding and ventured with caution, "Depends. Are you going to kill me for what I said earlier?"

"Right after I maim your brother for giving you my address," she promised sweetly, with just the hint of a smile.

He dropped the ridiculously heavy flowers onto the ground. "He didn't. I asked one of my investigators at the firm to dig up your info. Brian doesn't even know I'm here."

"Afraid to tell him?" she prodded with little sympathy.

"Shouldn't I be?"

Leaning against the doorframe, she took her sweet time answering, "Nah, Brian will probably just laugh his ass off."

That's what he was afraid of.

And clearly, the grinning imp darn well knew it, too.

Seeing her amusement at his expense ripen even more, he saw a brief opening and took a shot, "So are you going to put me out of my misery already and forgive me?"

"I don't know. Did you apologize?" she countered.

Damn, she wasn't going to make this easy for him.

"I'm...sorry, Abby. Truly." The words were rusty and foreign in his mouth; they weren't ones he used very often.

Suddenly, her smile dissolved into a look of remembered irritation. "Sorry for calling me a gold digging whore or for saying I was too fat to be in a trashy wet t-shirt contest?"

He reeled back as if bitch-slapped. "I didn't call you fat! Good lord, you don't really think that about yourself, do you?"

"Of course not," she snapped.

"Good." He wasn't a fan of women who were constantly putting themselves down. "If you did, I'd tell you to go get some new glasses. Your body's gorgeous."

She bristled in disbelief. "I'm not some self-conscious girl in need of your validation, you big twerp. I *laugh* when my dress size stays in the double digits during holiday months; it means my friends and family put that much more love into their dishes that year. I don't need false compliments from a guy who dates size zero models to feel good about myself."

He shot his hands in the air like a good little gunfire target. "It wasn't a false compliment. What I said back at my house was the lie—if any of it had been even remotely true, I wouldn't have said it. I'm not a cruel person. The fact that I did say it meant it was the furthest thing from the truth, which made it a safe insult."

Doing his damndest to keep his eyes from drifting

down to said gorgeous body, he admitted in complete honesty, "Truth is, you were so unbelievably sexy in that wet t-shirt earlier, I could hardly bear it."

Even now, the lingering memory of how she'd looked with the soaked fabric plastered to her smoking hot body was more than he—and the fit of slacks—could bear.

She paused long enough for him to see about five different emotions flit across her face before she eventually landed on one...and exploded.

"You are SO annoying! Are you really trying to turn an insulting, objectifying, insanely illogical comment like that into a half-baked compliment?!"

He grinned. "Is it working?"

"No!" But she couldn't completely tamp down the smile that was obviously trying to escape.

She really did have a great smile.

Danger, Connor Sullivan, danger. He was getting sucked in by her all over again. "So, where should I put these?" he asked levelly, picking up the flowers again to avoid looking at her. "Over on that table by the window?"

"And have it block all the light in my living room?" she laughed, opening the door all the way to let him in, seemingly unaffected by the electricity he felt buzzing between them. "I guess you can put it on the kitchen table; I'm pretty sure it's sturdy enough to handle the weight."

She gazed admiringly at the colorful assortment as he set it down. "Thank you, Connor. They're beautiful. Unnecessary, but appreciated all the same."

"They're entirely necessary," he said gruffly, rejoining her in the living room, "I was way out of line."

She lifted a shoulder. "You thought you were protecting Brian; I understand the compulsion, trust me."

Brian. The mental splash of ice-cold reality was just as effective today as it'd been the other night. Shoving his hands in his pockets, he switched over to small talk. "Yeah, he's one of the good ones. Have you two been dating long?"

She replied very…carefully, "What has Brian told you?"

"Nothing at all, really. I was actually surprised to see you with him at the party." Stunned was more like it. Seeing Brian with any woman other than Beth had been an altogether surreal experience. "You look cute together."

Okay, now the shifty woman looked like she was chewing on an old wad of gum.

His eyes narrowed.

Had he been right in his accusations earlier? Maybe she'd just used Skylar as her cover. A very effective one.

"How serious are you about Brian? If you don't mind me asking."

With a quick glance at the clock, she evaded poorly, "Oh, look at the time. I've got a meeting to get to and I need to shower first."

She reopened the front door. Subtle.

"Thanks for the flowers, Connor. I accept your apology, of course."

Briskly ignoring his body's response to the image of her in the shower, he caught her by the elbow and crowded her against the wall.

"You're hiding something. What is it?"

She shook her head in denial and suddenly, the warm scent of chocolate assailed his senses.

His gaze dropped down to her lips. "Hot cocoa," he murmured. So the empty mug on the kitchen table hadn't been filled with coffee then.

Her response was barely a whisper. "I was cold."

His blood fired. Imagining all the ways he could've helped warm her up nearly brought him to his knees.

Tugging on her elbow once more, he pulled her body flush against his.

Jesus, every inch of her fit him perfectly.

Damn it.

CHAPTER FOUR

"I'M NOT POACHING my brother's woman," he rumbled in her ear, his words a hot, rough brand against her skin.

Abby shivered, arched her neck at the sensation. No, of course he wouldn't poach. Not Connor. She'd been hearing about Saint Connor for years now from both Brian and Beth. A bit of a man whore, yes, but an otherwise great guy.

A noble bad boy.

And all the more irresistible for it.

A large part of her reasoned she should set the record straight right now. Explain that she *wasn't* Brian's woman. Free Connor's guilty conscience.

Give the green light for the kiss they both wanted.

Instead, she turned her head away. "You should go."

His sharp inhalation cut the air like a knife as he backed quickly away from her. "Abby, I'm sorry. I didn't—"

The slamming of a car door had them jumping apart another three feet. Abby shifted her gaze to the driveway and saw Brian bounding toward them, sprinting through the rain.

Geez, when it rained it poured.

"Hey, Brian. What's up?"

"We just wanted to make sure you got home okay." He sluiced water off his jacket and pointed back to the SUV.

Seeing Skylar rapid-fire waving from the passenger seat, Abby smiled and waved back. "What's with all the worrying? You'd think this was acid rain I ran home in."

Instead of replying, Brian slid his attention over to Connor. "Skylar mentioned you might be here. Everything alright?"

"Never better." Connor's face was the picture of innocence. "Just checking in on Skylar's guardian angel here, same as you."

"Uh huh." Brian nodded over at her kitchen. "Nice flowers. Who died?"

Abby drew out a forlorn sigh. "The perils of ordering flowers online. Small summer bouquet, my ass."

Connor's shoulders shook in silent laughter.

Brian rolled his eyes. "You suck at lying." He turned

on his brother. "What'd you do?"

"Nothing!" Abby broke in, cutting Connor off at the pass. "It was just a small misunderstanding. No biggie."

Arms folded over his chest, Brian silently looked from her to Connor then back to her. "This misunderstanding wouldn't have anything to do with you and me would it?"

Abby shot Brian her loudest *shut the hell up* glare, knowing that the power of telepathy she'd secretly wished for as a kid was still on back order.

"You did the big brother thing, didn't you?" he sighed, shaking his head at Connor. "Did you grill her 'til she broke?"

Connor pinned her with a dark look. "I tried. But Abby apparently keeps secrets extremely well." Suspicion and something…weightier than distrust rolled off of him in waves.

Brian frowned. "Hey, ease up. I asked Abby to play along so you'd stop looking at me with such pity."

Connor snapped his gaze back over to Brian. "*What?* I haven't been doing that have I?"

"Yeah," Brian said softly, "you have. Look, I get it— my wife died, I'm a single dad of a preteen daughter, and my last date before Beth was at a bowling alley when I was fifteen. If the shoe were on the other foot, I'd be a pain in your ass too. But it's been a year; I'm doing fine. Better than fine. You've got to stop worrying so much about me."

"Not happening," grunted Connor. "It's all a part of

the sibling platinum package. And you have a lifetime membership."

Brian grinned. "I wasn't asking you to revoke my club card. Just…try to lay off the kid gloves around me, will you?"

Connor gave him another burly, noncommittal grumble that made Abby swoon just a tiny bit. If she were the type to keep a checklist for the dream-perfect guy, 'being a protective brother' would now be a top ten criteria. It was incredibly sexy.

And their manly bickering was just plain cute.

She smiled, half expecting a poignantly awkward bro hug at some point.

Unfortunately, she realized much too late to do any good that she wasn't just smiling, she was staring. At Connor.

And he was staring right back.

A slow smile transformed his expression, right before he abruptly asked the inevitable, "So that means the two of you…"

"—aren't really dating," shrugged Brian.

"*Interesting.*"

Lordy, Abby had heard of a 'wolfish grin' before, but no one told her it'd make her panties catch on fire.

She quickly moved to usher both brothers out of her doorway. "Well, since that's all settled, everyone can head on home and I can get back to that much-needed shower I never got to take."

Great, there was that wolfish grin again.

You just had to bring up the shower didn't you?

Connor was practically eating her up with his eyes. And she liked it. Far too much. So she chose to treat his heated stare like a solar eclipse and blindly push both men right off her porch back into the rain.

Eventually, they had no choice but to run back to their cars to avoid getting soaked.

And the very moment they were both out of sight, she rushed through her house to her bathroom, pulling her clothes off as she went.

Screw the shower, she needed a long, hot bath.

With some waterproof accessories.

She was stripped bare and just about done filling up the tub when her cell phone jangled from her bag in the bedroom.

Groaning, she hurried out to grab the phone, answering it on the way back into the bathroom without checking the caller id. "Hello?"

"That was a quick shower."

Abby almost fell headfirst into the tub.

Luckily, she managed to hang on to her wits though. "You know, I'm really starting to hate your investigator."

Connor chuckled. "Actually, Skylar gave me your cell phone number before I went to pick up the flowers. She figured I might need it in case you slammed the door in my face."

"So blood really is thicker than milkshakes," she

grumbled as she stomped over to the tub to shut off the water before it overfilled. "What do you want, Connor?"

"Now there's a loaded question."

The sigh she aimed at herself bounced off the tiled walls in stereo. She'd walked right into that one.

There was a brief silence over the phone line and then a very curious, "Are you talking to me from the bathroom?"

Oh my, Miss Manners would have a conniption. "Yes. But to be clear, I'm not *using* the bathroom or anything."

His quiet laughter was the stuff of bath-time fodder.

The deep sound went through her like whiskey as she perched on the tub edge and swished a lazy hand through the water.

She heard him suck in a soft breath. And every nerve in her body flared to life at the sound.

"You're taking a bath." His voice was a full octave lower, his tone almost reverent.

Startled, Abby looked around to check the walls for eyes. A pair of piercing blue eyes in particular...a distinctly sexy set that always looked deep in thought.

"No. Not yet, anyway."

Another pause. "So what's stopping you?"

"You."

Was it possible to hear someone smile?

"So because of me, your water's getting cold?"

"Exactly. Now if you'd hurry and tell me what you

want, I could get back to my bath before it gets any colder."

"Maybe what I want is to join you in the tub. What are the chances of that happening?"

"None to none at all." *Liar.*

He made a disappointed sound, but didn't give up that easily. "I promise I'll behave. Unless…you're going to do something in the bath that you'd need privacy for." He put just enough goading in his tone to tick her off, but not enough for her to hang up on him. "Is that the case?"

Yes. And the jerk was being deliberately obtuse about it.

She maintained radio silence.

"Because if that is the case, I don't *have* to behave. I could…misbehave."

Her jaw locked at his audacity.

A firm believer that one should never negotiate with terrorists, she decided to instead fight fire with fire. "Since it doesn't look like I'm getting rid of you anytime soon, I'm just going to go ahead and start…my bath."

She grinned in triumph when a quiet groan came from his end.

Placing her phone on the counter, she dropped her towel and slid into the water. The slow, purring sound she let out wasn't for his benefit.

But it seemed to affect him all the same.

"Am I on speaker?" The words were smoky, stilted.

"Mmm hmm." Her eyelids drifted closed as she sank

back against the tub, letting the hot water unravel the tension from this crazy day. "Connor, you have maybe a minute before I start dozing off so if you have something to say, you better say it now."

"Have dinner with me."

She bolted upright—to avoid taking in a gaping mouthful of bath water.

"*Dinner?* Why?"

"Because the next time you're in that tub, I want to be there with you. And, well, I figure it'd be wise for us to eat beforehand."

He was smiling again, she could hear it.

The guy had balls, she had to give him that. "What on earth makes you think I'd agree to take a bath with you?"

"Nothing but sheer hope."

She resisted the urge to melt at that, reminding herself that this was a veteran player she was talking to here.

And she'd barely even cut it in little league.

"I don't think dinner would be a good idea."

"Okay, lunch then. Afternoon baths are fun too."

Dang it, she was really close to laughing. "No. And don't you dare suggest breakfast or dessert. Or brunch!"

"Well then we have a problem. Call me old fashioned but I'd really like to feed you before we take a bath together."

Somehow, she managed to smother the life out of a

burgeoning giggle. "That was a blanket no. To the bath also."

"*Fine*. But you don't know what you're missing. I'll have you know, I give a pretty mean underwater massage."

Ooh, that was low. Her achy muscles wanted in. But her common sense knew better. "Oh, I believe you. I'd be more surprised if you told me you gave a nice one."

"Ouch. Okay, okay, I deserved that. Well, since you've now clearly moved on to the brutally honest portion of our phone call, why don't you explain why you told me to leave earlier?"

"Brian already covered all that," she skirted.

"So that was the only reason? Honoring that favor?"

God save her from insightful men. "Not exactly," she confessed. "It was just…easier to let you believe it."

"Easier than…"

"Saying no to you." She stared at the water, admitting quietly to herself as well as to him, "When all I wanted was to say yes."

"*Abby*."

It came out as a groan.

And sounded like pure sin.

She couldn't help it, in the thick quiet that followed, her hands began drifting over her skin without any preauthorization from her brain whatsoever.

Eyes closed, she let her fingers roam. Until her broken breathing fractured the silence.

"Invite me over, Abby," Connor rasped. "Let me see

you. Help you."

Her eyes shot open and she yanked her hands back to safer territory.

What the heck was she thinking?

"What? No."

"Why not?" His voice sounded strained.

"Because we just met!"

"No, we met well over a decade ago. And as you so delicately reminded me the other night," he added almost teasingly, "we've kept in fairly regular contact since."

She tried to keep her smile from showing in her voice. Why was it so easy to like this man? "You can't come over."

"Then at least agree to dinner, Abby. Just one night."

"Coming from you, Connor, that sounds less like a reassurance and more like a mandate."

Crap. She hadn't intended for that to sound so bitchy. She had no right to judge him. "Errr...not that that's a *bad* thing."

He was silent for a second. "Are you saying you've never had a one-night stand? Ever?" All their earlier playfulness was wiped clean from his voice.

"Nope."

But for once, she was tempted. Boy, was she tempted. "Besides, even if I were that kind of girl, I couldn't have one with you. Our lives are too connected. There's Brian and Skylar to think about."

Not to mention, you'd utterly break my heart.

"We both know it wouldn't be a good idea, Connor."

A resigned grumble vibrated over the phone line. "You're probably right."

"Sheesh, you don't have to be so upset about it...don't worry, I'll let you be right next time," she teased without thinking.

A big, surprised chuckle burst out of him. "If you want to take the sting out of this rejection you just handed out, you're going to have to work on being a hell of a lot less cute. And smart. The snappy comebacks are becoming a major turn on for me."

She bit her lip. That was just about the sweetest compliment she'd ever received. "You know, we can still be friends."

This time his laughter sounded almost regretful. "What'd I say about cutting down on the cuteness?"

"Is that a no?"

He sighed. "That's a maybe. Or at least an 'I'll try.'"

"I hate it when people say that," she complained. "It's such a copout."

"Well, it's the best you're going to get. 'I'll try' means I'm going to let you go finish your bath alone, and not hit on you again for at least another twenty-four hours."

She'd never been one to look a gift horse in the mouth. "Fine. You have a deal. For *now*. I'll work on wearing you down later."

"Funny, I was just about to say the same thing to you."

A strange thrill ran up her spine. "Goodbye, Connor."

"Bye Abby…and have a good bath."

"You too." She frowned. "Wait. That came out weird. I meant a good *one*; have a good one."

She paused again. Was it her or did that sound a little dirty?

Pinching her bridge of her nose, she tried again, "A good one as in a good time. Like I'm planning to have in the tub."

Jesus.

A double-shot of oxygen hissed past her teeth.

Flustered, she attempted one more fix, "Not that I'm implying you'll be doing what I'll be doing—"

Oh. Good. *Lord!*

He growled. "Twenty-four hours, Abby. We'll be 'friends' for twenty-four more hours and then you better believe we'll be having this conversation again."

She dunked her head under water as soon as he hung up, dazed at the prospect of resisting a man like Connor Sullivan.

Soon, *she* was the one spouting copouts.

CHAPTER FIVE

SHE WAS A COWARD. She'd spent the entire day working on her dissertation in the campus library instead of at home. *Just* in case Connor decided to call.

Not that she was under the fanciful impression that a big time lawyer like him had the time to be lounging around calling her all day.

Still, she liked to err on the side of caution.

And apparently, it was a good thing she did. Because when she finally threw in the towel and returned home at half past five, the shiny black Lexus awaiting her arrival confirmed yet again why cautious should've been her middle name.

"Busy day?" The question was casual, though Connor's expression was anything but.

She decided to try for facetious. "As I'm sure you're aware, stalking is a legally actionable offense in all fifty states."

"God, don't use legalese on me, Abby. Hearing it in your sexy teacher voice is just making it that much harder for me to stay your 'friend' for the next..." he checked his watch, "fifty-six minutes."

Oh it was no use, she smiled a little over that.

"Have you been hiding from me?" he asked abruptly, visibly upset. "I called you twice today. Both times, it went straight to voicemail."

"I was doing research. My cell phone doesn't get good reception in certain parts of the library."

"Oh."

Seeing him look noticeably eased by that information stuck her with a needle of guilt. What she said *was* all true, but not the whole truth. She'd spent the majority of her time on the special collections floor and the rest reading on the third floor where she could also eat—two areas of the library where, incidentally, her phone caught just fine. At least, when it was switched on.

"...And maybe I was avoiding you a tiny bit."

"I knew it." His eyebrows snapped together. "Are you afraid of me? Do I make you uncomfortable or something?"

"I think it's more a case of my being *too* comfortable with you." She blew out a weary breath, knowing that only made sense to her. "Look, I'm not afraid of you. In fact, why don't you come in and hang out? I can whip up some food and we can watch a DVD or some TV."

The look on his face was how she imagined an alien would look upon arriving on a new planet. It would have been funny if it weren't a bit sad.

She unlocked her door and went in, leaving him free to enter or leave. "You said we could be friends for another hour, right? So come on. I can tell you all about my day hiding out from my stalker."

Finally, he broke out into a grin and followed her inside, making the temperature in the tiny foyer they were standing in even balmier when he removed his suit jacket.

Lord, the man had a broad chest.

Great arms, too.

"Sorry, I'll get the AC going. You can grab a beer from the fridge if you want. I was thinking of making some steak fajitas and a salad," she called out as she made her way to the bedroom to change. "That okay with you?"

"Sounds great."

She came back out in an old t-shirt and sweats, purposely choosing not to pretty up for Connor.

Oddly, he seemed to appreciate that fact, judging by the pleased smile he gave her when she returned. "Do you need help cooking? I want to earn my meal."

"Sure. Can you fry up the flank steak for me? The meat is marinating in a ziploc in the fridge."

She was surprised at how normal she sounded, what with his presence seemingly sucking up all her usual oxygen supply in the kitchen. Her whole house, really, if she was being honest with herself.

Damn, when was that AC going to kick in?

"Hey, are you going to have enough food for me too?" asked Connor as he poked around in her fridge. "Because I can always just eat a ham and cheese or PB&J."

The thought of this high-powered attorney with his head to toe dry clean only ensemble eating a brown bag sandwich served to finally calm her nerves down. "I always make extra for leftovers the next day so it'll be fine."

She started cutting up a few avocados to make some fresh guacamole. "Cilantro, onions, and tomatoes okay in the guac? I make mine chunky."

"Perfect. Brian makes it the same way."

"He would. I'm the one who got him hooked on it."

Connor tilted his head at that tidbit as he threw the meat in the skillet. "I still find it so hard to believe I don't have any recollection of seeing you after that first day at the hospital."

She went with a breezy, unoffended shrug. "Guess I just have one of those forgettable faces."

He gave her a quiet look. "No, you don't. My point, exactly."

Good lord, so *that's* what a 'smoldering glance' looked like? With Connor's ice blue eyes, the effect was lethal to her lady parts.

"Well, it's not as if the times we saw each other in passing were momentous events," she recovered, just barely stopping herself from telling him how unforgettable she'd always found him. "Plus, family gatherings for siblings and friends to meet and hang out weren't really your parents' sort of thing."

"No," he snorted, "unless you count the occasional $500 a plate fundraising dinners. Which I don't."

"Honestly, I think we only actually 'saw' each other the couple of times there was some emergency requiring us to do a Skylar hand-off at Brian's house."

"That explains it," he said quietly.

Abby knew what he meant. Each time she'd run into him, the fact that he'd looked criminally handsome had hardly even had a chance to register. Not with everything Beth was going through hanging on them like a dark cloud—the heftiness of why they'd been on opposite sides of a lonely two-way road to and from Brian's house so often to begin with.

"Was it as hard for you to go there as it was for me?" she asked softly.

"Yes." He looked up from the stove. "My mother never went over enough to get it, and as cold as it sounds, I don't know if my father really cared enough to either."

With a heavy sigh, he turned the steak over and murmured, "You know, Skylar called me 'dad' once."

To anyone outside of the conversation, the comment would seem totally random.

But she got it.

Stark, bleak sympathy kicked her in the gut as she

admitted in an equally saddened tone, "Skylar called me mommy a few times, too. Twice, Beth heard it."

The frustration-laden curse under his breath was an all too familiar one for her too, as the only f-bombs she ever dropped almost exclusively had the word Huntington's strapped to it.

It was a sad comfort to have someone else around that knew exactly what the last decade had been like for her as Brian's best friend.

After a long, heavy silence, Connor eventually looked up at her again with a speculative glance. "Hey, what about Skylar's third birthday party?" he asked, his tone now several tons lighter. "The pool party?" His eyes made a slow pass over her, the return trip back up lingering in places that made her think of sexy supervillains with flame-throwing gazes. "You in a swimsuit? There is just no way I could've seen that and not remembered."

If it was possible, his hot look scorched ten degrees higher when it settled back on her eyes.

Luckily, the very vivid memory of that party was funny enough to prevent her from succumbing to a heat stroke. "I think you had your hands full that day."

He looked genuinely puzzled by that.

"Oh, to be an archived entry in your little black book," she tsked. "Or should I say entr*ies*."

Slow understanding dawned in his eyes. "Shit, I forgot about that."

"Yup, you made that admission a few times that

day." And the resulting reality show worthy catfight at the pool had been colossal.

He cringed. "To be fair, I didn't actually *invite* either of those women to that party." His tone turned innocent. "Just like I didn't invite the woman I was dating at the time, either."

Shaking her head, she began setting the food on the coffee table. "No wonder you have the reputation you do."

"I don't *have* a reputation." He brought over the steak and their bottles of beer, correcting her with a grin, "I *earned* it."

Abby burst out laughing. "You're kind of an ass, you know that, right?" The rest of her laughs got lodged in her throat when she turned and practically ran right into him.

Holy swizzle sticks, did he have to be so *masculine*?

"But you like me anyway," he prodded in that low, melting Vegas hypnotist voice, leaning in without any regard for her personal space. "Despite my ass-likeness."

So close. He was so close she could bury her face against his neck if she wanted. Breathe him in whether she wanted to or not. "No," she lied, backing up a step since it was clear he had no intention of doing so. Yep, an ass for sure.

One she wanted to rub up against like a cat finding her purr.

She took another ginormous step back.

He followed, invading her sanity even more than before. "No? So what do I have to do to change that?"

Christ, he wasn't even *trying* yet?

"Alright, alright, so I like you. Why wouldn't I? We're friends, right?" It'd do a world of good to remind herself, too. With a big, *friendly* smile, she sidestepped him and gestured back over to the coffee table. "C'mon, let's eat. Sit. The food's getting cold."

At first, she felt a twinge of disappointment when he conceded and reluctantly backed away…until she heard his husky, murmured caveat, "Fifteen more minutes, Abby."

The time remaining in their friend truce.

She held strong, refusing to let her imagination run with what exactly the man could do in fifteen minutes otherwise.

But then he had to go and tuck a throw pillow behind her as she sat down, fluff it for her to make sure she was comfortable.

Not to win points.

Rather, just because he was *that* guy.

The unconsciously sweet bad boy.

Now why'd she insist on this truce again?

CHAPTER SIX

CONNOR COULDN'T BELIEVE he was sitting on a living room floor eating dinner with Abby. He hadn't done something like this since college.

It was…nice.

"So besides hiding from me, what were you doing in the library today?"

She gave him a shy smile. "One of my dissertation research questions focuses on the swinging pendulum of business and technical writing instruction throughout history. My research has unearthed some pre-college cases after the technology boom—a few pivotal high school cases as early as the 1900s. To contrast these findings with the present, I've been collecting data from school resources all across Arizona."

She was speaking so fast now, it was kind of adorable.

"You know, I've even found old teaching materials that are strikingly similar to current trends, though they're rarely linked in scholarly articles. And amazingly, each instance that's impacted the pedagogical foundation of today's technical writing landscape correlates directly to societal goings-on at the time. It's fascinating."

Oh yeah, she was an academic alright, through and through. He grinned at the pink in her cheeks. Not quite the type of passion he'd been hoping to inspire in her, but moving just the same.

"What's wrong?" he asked when she didn't continue; she'd been on such a roll.

She gnawed on her lip. "Sorry, I know this all sounds boring and nerdy to...well, any normal person. You've actually lasted longer than most of my friends and family. Their eyes would've been glazed over by my second sentence."

The way she smiled at him—like he was a foot taller than he'd been a minute ago—filled him with an inordinate amount of pleasure.

"On the contrary, a lot of what you said was pretty thought-provoking." He gave her a reassuring grin. "Don't get me wrong, some of your explanations did bear an uncanny resemblance to the college lectures I used to somehow take notes in without any conscious brain involvement," he teased, "but your passion kept me engaged in everything you were saying. It's obvious you're a good teacher."

There was that smile again. If she kept it up, he'd be growing in other ways too.

She shook her head and focused on assembling another fajita. "You know, you're nothing like I expected."

"I'm glad you gave me a chance to redeem myself."

Her brows rose at the reminder. "Yeah, what was with that freak-out at your house yesterday? It seemed a little...excessive."

He took his time chewing his food, trying to phrase his answer in the least offensive way. "Let's just say women showing up at my home half-dressed isn't exactly an unusual occurrence for me."

"Right, of course. That happens a lot on this street too." She chortled. Mostly at his expense.

Of all the different facets to Abby's personality, Connor decided he liked the feisty one the best. "Don't laugh. You'd be surprised what lengths some women will go to seduce a man they've built up in their heads."

She leaned over and butted his shoulder with her own. "Oh, don't get all modest on me now. We both know you probably live up to every expectation these women have of you."

His smiled faded and he turned to face her fully. "Don't."

Startled, she looked up at him. "Don't what?"

"Don't go thinking I'm someone I'm not."

Studying him carefully, she replied as if she were teaching something so obvious to a five-year old, "I won't if you won't. Sounds to me like you think a lot less of yourself than you should."

It was a compliment wrapped in a slap upside his head, and it had him actually wanting to be that man she seemed to see.

Of course, figuring out how such a man would respond to her shut-up-and-accept-it admiration of him, however, had him stumped. His normal reply would've been of the pulling-off-her-clothes variety.

He was guessing that wasn't the right response here.

She cleared her throat, probably to bring his eyes back up from her bare shoulder. How the woman managed to look so sexy in a huge, beat-up men's football tee was beyond him. "I'm sorry. I didn't hear what you just said."

Her look told him she *knew* he was anything but sorry. "I asked why you were so convinced I was a gold-digger. You're a handsome guy, couldn't a wet t-shirt wearing woman on your porch step just be after you for sex? The uniform would suggest so."

He shrugged. "Most of the ones who've shown up have been. But if I were broke off my ass, they wouldn't have been standing at my door to begin with."

"Point taken." She chewed thoughtfully. "So you're saying the only women who you deign to let in your home are the ones who aren't interested in your money at all?"

"If I did, I'd have to take a vow of celibacy," he

replied honestly. "It's a catch-22. Typically, the women not interested in my money are also not interested in a one-month arrangement."

"Ah yes, the infamous one-month Connor Sullivan rule. Brian's told me about it. I bet that's another factor for some of these women who throw themselves at you—trying to become the white unicorn who you one day break your rule over."

His jaw firmed. "Never going to happen."

The corner of her lips quirked up. "Don't worry, stud. I'm not submitting an application or anything."

Now why did that declaration fill him with a touch of disappointment?

"Enough about me," he said gruffly. "Tell me more about you. Something besides your research."

She laughed. "Well that narrows it way down. Now that I'm in my final year of my PhD program and done with all my coursework, my dissertation is the only big thing in my life right now. Other than that, there's really not much to tell."

"What about work? Don't you tutor at Skylar's school?"

"Oh, I do that as a volunteer. A couple of afternoons a week for the kids that are struggling."

How noble. He couldn't remember the last woman he'd met whose idea of volunteering wasn't strictly confined to sitting on an executive board or planning a fundraising event. "I could've sworn Brian told me you teach English."

"I do. I teach English full-time at ASU as a part of my fellowship. I get my tuition covered and get paid a lecturer's salary, which isn't much. Thankfully, I'm saving a ton of money renting out this guesthouse from one of my professors. Living here costs way less than what I used to pay for my apartment in Tempe two years ago. And, I basically get this entire half of their big ole lot all to myself."

Connor leaned back, stuffed, surprised at how easy it was to talk with Abby. "Doesn't sound like you have that much time for yourself. What do you do for fun?"

She got up to grab them another two beers from the kitchen. "Honestly, I'm a homebody. Never got into the nightlife scene here. Plus, by the time I was twenty-one, I was basically babysitting Skylar all day every weekend, and nearly all my weeknights. Since that pretty much carried on clear until last year, I guess my idea of fun is hanging out with her. Lame, I know."

He felt like he was talking to a martian.

He hadn't realized she'd spent even more time babysitting Skylar than he had. Tons more. And he knew for a fact—from Brian's complaints about it—that she hadn't taken a single cent from them for babysitting.

For God's sakes, she was just so *nice*.

"So you don't do anything just for yourself? Just for you, just for fun?"

"Well, I have been privately executing my mission

to learn how to cook the most beloved dishes from every country in the world," she returned with a big smile as she plopped back down on the ground. "That's fun."

It was possible baby bluebirds helped her get dressed in the morning.

She was just that sweet.

"You're driving me crazy." He swept an arm around her waist and lifted her right up onto his lap.

"Connor!"

He slid a hand into her hair, rubbed a thumb over her heated cheekbone as he brought his lips to within inches of hers. "I shouldn't want you this much. You're everything I'm not, and I'm everything you couldn't possibly want. I know I should leave you alone, but I just can't. I can't stop myself from wanting you."

Her breathing had grown so erratic, he was actually starting to get concerned. "Say something, sweetheart. I'm baring my soul here."

"I shouldn't want you either," she whispered, "but I do."

His arms locked around her, instinctively staking a claim on her.

Mine.

For now.

The two words were his only anchor keeping him in the reality he maintained for himself. He had to be brutally honest with her, with them both. "I meant what I said earlier, Abby. I'm never going to break my one-month rule." Feeling like the lowest piece of scum, he hammered that last nail in, "Not for anyone. Not even you."

She was silent for a long while, and Connor started preparing himself for the rejection to come.

"I know our fifteen minutes of friendship are up but can I ask you something as a friend? Will you answer me as one?"

He tensed. "I'll try."

She chuckled. "Again with the copout." Raising her warm doe eyes up to his, she asked quietly, "If you weren't trying to get in my pants, if you were just my friend and I asked you what one thing I could do to stop being 'a nice girl' for just a little while, what advice would you give me?"

That was easy. "I'd tell you to try something new. Something that excites you. Something that'll take you from zero to sixty just as fast as it could take you back to zero whenever you were ready to return."

"Something wild and fast..." She loosened her death grip on his shoulders, slid her hands down his back slowly. "That's good advice."

He saw her gaze travel down to his lips and it took everything he had not to kiss her right then and there.

"Are you volunteering, Connor? To be that something wild and fast for me to try?"

"No," he replied raggedly, "I'm insisting. Requiring." He dropped his forehead against hers. "Asking."

Her eyelids dipped down, completely veiling her

reaction from him.

So he waited.

"I can't do a whole month with you."

He blinked in surprise. *That,* he hadn't been expecting. "Why not?!"

"It's too long."

Well, he did ask.

A touch indignant, he argued, "You said you don't do one-night stands. Now you're saying that a month is *too long*?"

He knew he was getting overly worked up but he couldn't help it, she was being irrational. His brain started firing on all pistons, every combat cell in his body taking a front seat like they always did when he was about to do battle in the courtroom. "Or is it just one month with *me* that's too long?"

She flinched.

He felt thoroughly insulted.

"It's not how you're making it. Being with you would be like...ice cream. The most decadent ice cream I could ever imagine. I'd be hooked after the first bite. And if I didn't discipline myself, I'd...overindulge."

"Until it made you sick?" He wasn't really good with metaphors.

A smiled peeked through. "No, until it was all I'd want to eat, all day, every day."

What the hell was wrong with that?

Her smile broadened. "There's everything wrong

with that," she continued, somehow reading his mind. "One month will take me right up to the third week of teaching, which is generally when my life starts getting busy. That means this month is my only time to really focus on getting a huge chunk of my dissertation written."

"And if you overindulge on the ice cream…"

"I'd be in a sugar coma, incapable of doing or thinking of anything else. But you."

Call him a bastard but hearing that felt good. "Fine, I can respect that. How about this? What if I promise to leave you alone all day, every day throughout the week, and only send you into mini ice cream comas at night…as a build-up to one massive, no holds barred weekend to overindulge until we're both too weak to move? Would that work for you?"

Hot, slick desire exploded in her expression.

His fingers instantly flexed against her hips in response.

"Stand down, counselor. You made your point."

If she agreed to this arrangement, Connor fully intended to have her bring this legal speak into the bedroom—coming from Abby's lips it was the equivalent of dirty talk.

"How about we reach a compromise?" She caught her lower lip between her teeth. "Two weeks."

Two weeks? She was *negotiating?*

He didn't like it. Not one bit. "Half? You're only willing to give me half?"

Geez, he was doing a remarkable impression of a screech-fest he'd heard in the firm's conference room the other day.

"What's the big deal?" Now she looked genuinely mystified. "The one month is your maximum time period, isn't it? What's wrong with two weeks?"

Technically, nothing.

In reality, everything.

Though he wasn't quite sure why. As he mulled it over, he contemplated temporarily agreeing to the two weeks and then appealing midway for an extension...

Why the hell was he strategizing this like it was a court case?

"Will there be a possibility for extension?"

She frowned. "Wouldn't that defeat the purpose of these relationship parameters of yours?"

It would, yes. "I'll make an exception...unless you disclose a history of flipping out on the guys you date."

She winged an eyebrow up. "What if I did?"

Hell, he'd probably date her anyway.

What was it about her?

"I'll worry about that if it happens." He smiled when she did, and then proceeded to renegotiate—an occupational reflex. "How about we do a month, and lessen it to two weeks if you feel you really want to?"

He could tell she was trying not to grin.

Eventually, she sighed. "Even if I wanted to agree to those terms, I couldn't. I'm heading out of town the day after tomorrow for two weeks."

Something unsettling pricked inside of him. Unease? No, it stung deeper than that. Burned, actually.

Whatever it was, he wanted to be rid of it. "You're going on a trip? I thought you said you were busy."

"It's not a trip so much as me going home to stay with my parents for two weeks. My landlords are enclosing that huge patio off the kitchen to make an extra bedroom. They're slowly making this guest house bigger since I'll only be living here until next May, and their son is moving in with his wife and two kids after I'm gone."

"So they're kicking you out for two weeks? They should be providing you with an alternative place to live. It's standard for a landlord—"

She threw her palms in the air. "Whoa. Don't turn into Mr. Bigshot Lawyer. I offered to go home to California. Plus, they went out of their way to get a crew that could do the work really quick, specifically in these two weeks to fit my schedule. They even had the builders work out a plan where all the interior reno work would be completed before a lot of the less-pressing exterior projects, contrary to their normal construction routine, so all the more invasive parts would be taken care of before I got back. They really are being great about this."

"But everything you need for your research is here." He was well aware that he was pulling at threads now.

"True. But, the UC schools have an outstanding library system so I don't think I'll have too much difficulty accessing things. And at this portion of my write-up, a lot of what I need is online so I can easily take care of it in Santa Clara."

"But you'll lose half a day flying each way." Okay, *now* he was reaching rock bottom. He was actually embarrassed for his law school diploma; it was probably getting ready to jump off his office wall in protest.

"I'm not flying, I'm driving. It's peak travel season and flying over would cost more than I'd care to spend."

"You can't be serious." Now he was more concerned than argumentative. "You're planning on driving all the way to Santa Clara in that hunk of junk out in your driveway?"

"Hey!"

"Sorry, that very lovely POS 'SUV' out there."

She kept right on glaring at him.

Okay, so maybe it wasn't entirely necessary for him to have included the air quotes, but really, the vehicle was more like a very tall, beat up clown car than an SUV, circa never-bothered-to-be-recorded.

"Face it, that thing is a nine-car pileup waiting to happen. You shouldn't take it on that long of a road trip and you know it."

"Well, it's my only option right now."

Something occurred to him then. "Wait, if you knew you were going to be gone, why did you counter with two weeks?"

He detested false bids.

Her bottom lip disappeared between her teeth. "Actually, I meant the two weeks after I get back, before my schedule starts getting busy."

Wow, now he knew exactly how his previous one-monthers felt when he used to schedule them in.

"Sorry, that sounds terrible."

"No, it's fine. I've actually done the very same thing before." And he wouldn't ever be doing it again. This feeling was flat-out wretched. "Why don't you just find another place to stay here in town the next two weeks? It'd be simpler than traveling, and we'd still get to have the full month."

Good lord, why was he chasing the woman?

Though she did look supremely tempted, after a moment of thought, she still shook her head. "I can't impose on any of my friends for that long. And while I could just book a room somewhere for two weeks and end up spending about as much as I would on gas, I'd hate to try writing for that long in a hotel."

He studied her for a second before coming to a decision.

"Well...then stay with me."

CHAPTER SEVEN

STRUCK DUMB, and apparently deaf as well, Abby opened and closed her mouth once before shaking her head. Hard.

"*What?*" She must have heard him wrong. Must have.

"You heard me."

Did she?

Since Connor looked both pleased with himself and just a tiny bit like he might be ready to hurl, she assumed she had.

"I can't stay with you for two weeks."

"Why not?"

"Connor, be reasonable."

"I'm being very reasonable. Were you going home

to see your family or just to work on your dissertation?"

"The latter mostly," she confessed.

"Then do that at my house. I'm not there three-quarters of the time, anyway. And you can head to the library in the afternoons if you're worried about Skylar bothering you when she comes over after school…though it sounds like she and Brian have a pretty strict pact to leave you alone the next few weeks." He looked at her strangely. "You didn't tell them you were leaving did you?"

"I was working up to it. We have a fairly unhealthy codependent relationship."

He smiled. "So it seems. Even more reason to remain close by. C'mon, Abby, say yes."

"I really shouldn't."

"You'll have your run of the house. I'll stick to all aforementioned ice cream parameters. And you won't have to run around searching for that one mechanic in Arizona that might still be able to find parts for your car when you inevitably have to tow it off the freeway."

The man did make a good, if slightly brutal point.

"You'll have your own guestroom way on the other end of my—what is it you and Skylar call my house again?"

"The mini McMansion."

He chuckled. "Right. Well, you'll have your very own McSuite."

"And my own in-house McStud?"

"I do want to ensure you a quality stay," he deadpanned right back.

"Connor, this is crazy. This goes against everything you base your one rule on to begin with."

"Tell me the truth," he pressed, "if you could have a guarantee that it wouldn't be weird, would you stay? Would it help you with your research, and schedule, and sanity if you could just stay in town instead of driving all the way to California?"

She sighed, sounding exhausted even to her own ears. "Yes."

His face changed a little then, gentled, became serious. "Pretend we could rewind the clock back a half hour. You've been my brother's best friend for over a decade, basically a second mother to my niece, and the only one outside of family who helped my sister-in-law through her toughest times."

He gazed into her eyes with open honesty and candid respect. "There's not a single person on my speed dial more deserving of an invite to stay in my home than you. Let me do this. Let me help you with a place to stay for a few weeks so you can work on your dissertation and achieve the goals that you've managed to work toward in what little time you've spared for yourself. Stay with me. I mean it. It won't be weird."

So unfair. He was playing the noble big brother card and the sweet guy card—the two trump cards—at the same time.

When she still couldn't quite get herself to agree, he reached in his pocket and pulled out his cell phone.

"Who're you calling?"

"Brian. I'll have him convince you."

Alarmed, she grabbed for his phone. "No. Don't do that. I'd rather he and Skylar not know about…this."

A hopeful grin lit his face. "So there's a 'this' between us now?"

She shoved his phone back into his pocket. "It appears there is."

"Does this mean I can go ahead and start putting your luggage in my car?"

"IF I decide to do this, *I'll* be putting my luggage in *my* car and driving over to your place tomorrow."

"As long as you're sure your car will make it that far."

She pinched his arm.

He chuckled and gave her a reassuring smile. "I promise, if you hate it at my house, I'll have my mechanic look at your car so you can drive it all the way to California."

"You don't have to do that." She didn't *want* him to do that. She didn't want him spending money on her the way he did his other women. "My car is fine."

"I could always call Brian to ask him what he thinks about you driving that insurance risk on wheels over state lines."

Glaring at him, she huffed, "You don't play fair at all."

"Nope. That's actually the tagline on my business

card." He winked.

Sugarplums, a man this hard should *not* have such a playful, sexy wink. What was the universe thinking when they'd allowed that combination in his genetic makeup?

She mulled over the situation.

Or at least convinced herself she was, even though deep down she knew she'd already been ready to say yes after his moving speech about her goals. "If you're sure it won't get weird, I'd very much appreciate you letting me stay at your house, Connor. Thank you."

He flashed her a boyishly happy grin, one Abby hadn't seen on him yet. Thankfully. Because the effect was almost overkill on the man.

With the contrast of his sexy, espresso dark hair— almost black in this light—and his shockingly blue eyes that looked so hauntingly deep at times, the man was a danger to female kind the world over.

If she didn't take the appropriate measures, her heart would be joining their ranks on the endangered list.

"Just one thing... I'll only stay if we can agree that there will be no sex while I'm there."

———◆———

CONNOR ALL BUT TORE out of skin. "Why the hell not?"

"You know why. Do you really need me to go into detail about how hard it's going to be for me? For you?

Every day? What would the next morning in your house be like if we indulged in an all-night mind-blowing sexfest?"

The erection that had been battling for control ever since he'd first pulled Abby onto his lap roared to life, seeking someplace hot and slick to bury itself.

And not just any place.

Unable to help himself, he bucked his hips between Abby's legs in reflex. Because she was straddling him now. To prove her point.

"Because of *this*. Right here, Connor."

He grew another hard inch as her thighs clenched around his hips.

"We won't be able to control this and you know it."

He did know it. And it sucked.

"Fine," he agreed roughly, feeling like he was signing over the lease to his sanity with the concession.

She slid off his lap slowly, the barely tamed, hungry look in her eyes nearly his undoing.

"If that's going to be the terms of your stay, you better not plan on writing the day you're allowed to move back here, sweetheart," he growled. "Because after two weeks of *this*, I'll make damn sure your research is the last thing on your mind."

A look of hope lit her eyes. "Does that mean you're still going to give me my wild and fast, after the fact?"

Her breath broke so sweetly that he found himself groaning, "Fast is going to be a given, honey. At least the first three or four times that day, whether I want it to be or not."

A wobbly laugh escaped her. "I meant is it really okay with you that our one month is going to be different than what you're used to?"

"It'll be worth it," he assured her.

She stared at him for a weighty moment before getting up and scurrying onto the couch, leaving him on the floor, a good two feet away.

That was probably wise.

Didn't mean he had to like it. He picked up his beer and downed half the bottle. The liquid was already lukewarm but considering how unbelievably hot he was feeling, it was practically ice cold going down his throat.

"So what kind of case are you working on right now?"

He choked and almost sent the beer down the wrong tube.

She wanted to do small talk? Now?

One look at her was confirmation enough that she was serious. Sitting there with her forearms wrapped around her legs, knees tucked under her chin, and eyes still slightly glazed with arousal, she was seriously asking him about work.

"It's just that I figured you must be working on some big case since your phone has been going off nonstop in your pocket all night." Her eyes widened then as she turned her focus quickly down at her toes.

He grinned...because they both knew his phone had been on vibrate during all those missed calls.

And she'd been sitting on it for a good five minutes.

"Actually, I have been working on a big case," he eventually replied, letting her off from the teasing he was dying to give.

Just this once.

He turned and draped his arm on the seat cushion beside her, grinning outright when the accidental brush of his fingers against her calf had her eyes dilating sharply. "It's my most important one this year—a corporate acquisition tied to a multi-layered merger that I've spent months trying to close."

She frowned and sat up. "Why didn't you say something? You didn't have to waste the last hour eating here with me. And why the heck have you been ignoring all your calls?"

"I'd hardly call the last hour a waste of time. In fact, it's the most fun I've had in a while."

Clearly, she was unconvinced.

"As for my phone," he hesitated, and then went with the truth. "My work phone isn't on vibrate. The phone calls that I've been ignoring are from my, uh, personal cell."

"But what if it's Brian calling or... Ohhh." She looked away. "*That* kind of personal cell."

He felt like the world's biggest creep.

But he didn't want Abby to have any illusions about

him. "The last woman I dated isn't taking the end of our one month well. But it *is* completely over, I assure you. I'm not dating her or anyone else right now, in case you were wondering."

"I wasn't. Wondering, that is. I know you wouldn't be asking me for a month if you were."

He was utterly curious as to why, how she was so sure of such a thing.

At his questioning look, she shrugged. "You strike me as a monogam*ish* kind of guy. Plus, I don't believe you'd go through the hassle of enforcing a rule if you weren't going to be man enough to honor it yourself."

There was a good chance he was going to start needing this woman as a valium for his soul.

She saw a glimmer of good in even his worst qualities, and didn't hesitate to call him on the rest. But in a matter-of-fact way, free of judgment.

If it was possible, she seemed to just like him for being him.

"Hey," she said, concern latent in her voice. "You okay? You looked a little worried there for a second. Is it your case? Did you want to talk about it?"

She had to stop.

He couldn't take much more of her innate niceness; he didn't deserve it, didn't have the first clue what to do with it. "Oddly enough, I do want to talk about my case with you. Hell, I want to share my whole day with you. Which is why I *need* to do this."

So quickly it surprised even him, he swooped onto the couch and lowered his mouth down to hers.

Just one taste.

He just wanted one little taste before his hunger got out of control. Before he started craving things he couldn't truly have.

Like a nice girl he had no business wanting.

He stopped himself mere seconds before his lips made contact though...shut his eyes and took a steadying breath. Then another. And then finally backed away.

Christ, that was close.

But just when he'd gotten a handle on his roiling emotions, just when he thought he could be the good guy for a change, he felt two gentle hands smooth over the sides of his face.

And he was lost.

Because that was when *she* kissed *him*. Just once. Softly. Not at all like how he'd intended to kiss her, not at all like he normally kissed, period.

Yet it was the most memorable kiss he'd ever experienced.

"Just because we can't have sex doesn't mean you can't keep trying to convince me otherwise," she murmured against his lips.

Hot damn.

Everything male in him lit up to all systems go. He blinked down at her smiling face, not sure whether to be amused or turned on. Past experience dictated the two were mutually exclusive emotions for him.

Not so with Abby. "You're that confident in your ability to resist me?"

"Of course not. But resisting you and sticking to what I say I'm going to do are two completely different things."

"How do you figure?"

"I could, and very likely may fail at the first, but there isn't anything you could possibly do to make me fail at the second."

Brushing his lips gently against hers in a barely-there tease for them both, he whispered back in a thick voice he hardly recognized, "Challenge accepted."

He'd never been good with folks telling him there was something he couldn't do.

She smiled. "I was simply stating a fact. But if you want to take it as a challenge, feel free. Just so you know, if you do, it becomes a two-way street." So saying, she slid open those long curvy legs of hers and pulled him flush against her body. "Still up for the challenge?"

Now, he wasn't so sure.

A second later, she was kissing him again and he definitely wasn't sure.

The way she kissed…hell. It wasn't that she did some fancy new tongue trick or anything like that. It was just…nice.

And outrageously arousing.

"I better go pack," she said abruptly, pulling away

well before he was ready for the kiss to end. "I'll see you in the morning, Connor. Thanks for being my dinner company tonight. It was fun for me, too."

With that, she gave him a final kiss goodbye and stood up, by all accounts in total control of her senses.

Unlike him.

Well, shoot.

There was a *chance* this was going to be harder than he thought.

CHAPTER EIGHT

⎯⎯⎯✧⎯⎯⎯

"SO TELL ME, this bad boy reputation of yours—did it start in your personal life and bleed over into the courtroom or vice versa?"

Connor frowned as he helped Abby carry the last of her luggage up to his biggest guestroom, the only one that could accommodate the huge desk he'd relocated from his study.

At first, when she'd arrived at his house with three gigantic suitcases, he'd been shocked and a bit disillusioned. She hadn't seemed the type.

But now that he saw them each flipped open and filled to the brim with books and folders, and stacks of Xeroxed sheets and scribbled notes, he realized the small duffle bag on her shoulder was the only thing *not* carrying her research.

Now that seemed much more Abby.

He belatedly considered the question she'd asked. "That depends on who's doing the commenting about my reputation, I guess. Why?"

"I just wanted to see how accurate I was. Seems you have an unofficial coalition who thinks your licentious ways are going to be your downfall at the firm. I argued it couldn't possibly be, not with those very qualities being the ones that turned you into the kickass lawyer that's probably bringing in more money than over half the other lawyers there." She smirked at the memory. "I don't think those women like me very much now."

He leaned against the dresser and scowled, upset not on his behalf but hers. "Who were they? Was this on the night of the cocktail party?"

"Yup. A small group of corporate wives, one of whom I think might be an actual vampire, all rushed over to warn me away from you almost immediately after they saw you talking to me."

He discharged an irritated breath.

Cassandra and her minions. She was more a shewolf than a vampire but it was still an apt description.

She certainly had a reputation for sucking men dry.

Why his colleague Edward had thought it prudent to become husband number three for her was a complete mystery. "I don't get why those women gossip about me. I'm not really all that interesting."

"They seem to disagree. They went on and on about pool hall brawls and sex clubs."

He rolled his eyes. "The first is only partly true and the second not at all."

"Aw. Brian will be so disappointed," she teased. "He's been making cracks about all your sexual conquests for at least the last decade or so."

Oh, he has, has he?

He made a mental note to kick Brian's ass later. "Yeah, well my brother tends to have a flair for the dramatic."

"Really?" Another impish grin. "So no plundering or pillaging to speak of?"

Trust a future English professor to get him all hot and horny with choice vocabulary words. "Nope, sorry," he downplayed.

"I don't think I believe you," she sang out, hopping onto the bed and propping herself up on a pillow, heels kicking in the air as if they were about to exchange sleepover stories. "In fact, I think you're going to have to let me be the judge of that. Tell me the most supremely wicked thing you've ever done."

"I am *not* having this discussion with you."

"Why not?" She lowered her gaze down to his zipper, which seemed to be moving telekinetically. "Uncomfortable?"

He crouched over a bit more.

"C'mon. I'm curious about your hedonistic ways,"

she kept on, clearly amused by his discomfort. "Are we talking secret society orgies with whips and chains?"

"What?! God, no."

"Backdoor action? Threesomes?"

He averted his gaze to study a missed stitching in the rug he never noticed before.

"Seriously?" That quieted her, and boggled her eyes quite a bit. "Were they with two women or are you a 'Devil's Three Way' kind of guy?"

Where the hell did she learn that term? Attempting to clear his throat was suddenly very difficult. "Uh…both."

She let out a faint whistle. "Wow." Okay, she looked far too *curious* now for her own good.

"But I haven't done either in a while. It was all pretty much consolidated to one year of my life a long time ago."

"You didn't enjoy it?"

"I didn't say that." He shrugged. "Honestly, it was fun and exciting at the time but it got old fast. It's a ton more work than pornos make it out to be."

"Well, what if it were me and another girl satisfying your every carnal desire? Would you still feel like it was work?"

He nodded. And meant it. "Another woman would just end up getting in the way. Plus, she'd get all pissy that I'd be focusing solely on you and that's never fun."

She bit her lip, a reluctant smile peeking through regardless. "What a sweet, utterly disturbing compliment."

Her expression turned contemplative then. "Well what about you, me, and another guy?"

"Oh, *hell* no." He scowled. No way was he inviting some other man to see her, let alone touch her. A low growl rumbled in his chest.

No, just no.

The thought of it made him...jealous. An altogether unfamiliar and extremely unpleasant feeling.

"Oookay. Then how about the other thing? The...you know?" She turned a sweet shade of pink and shook her heinie in the air.

Holy hell, but the woman was trying to kill him. "Abby, you don't have to do any of that for me. Honest. Contrary to what the rumor mill spews out, I'm not some kinky sex fanatic. When you and I eventually get together, it's going to be plenty hot, believe me. We won't need any of those bells and whistles."

As he said it, he realized how true a statement that was. Just kissing Abby last night had been ten times more intoxicating than some of the more down and dirty romps he'd had with other women in his past.

"Hmm." She rolled over onto her back and stared up at the ceiling, silently thoughtful, a small smile playing on her lips.

Good god, what was she thinking now?

Already, this kinky interview from hell had him ten degrees past aroused. His own fault for coming in here, really. It was way past time for him to leave.

But just as he stood to go grab what was unequivocally going to be a very cold shower, Abby sat back up and called out casually, "Hey, could you toss me my lotion?" She pointed at the dresser behind him. "My legs get so dry here in the summers without it."

Such an innocent request.

That he didn't trust for one second.

He was sure this was going to be a look but don't touch deal with her lathering up those gorgeous legs of hers while he sat there like a schmuck.

Staring, no doubt.

He narrowed his eyes and began silently listing all the ways he was going to pay her back for this when her two-week stay here was up.

Slapping an unaffected look on his face, he passed her the lotion, forcibly blocking all the erotic lotion-inspired images that were attempting to take over his brain.

Evil woman.

Only a day into their no-sex agreement and already he was closer to begging than he cared to admit.

While avoiding direct eye contact with the skin smoothing extravaganza, his gaze strayed to the partially open plastic bag sitting atop her dresser. It was over at the other end but he recognized the hot purple logo on the bag immediately.

Just like that, every muscle in his body stopped working.

Well, save one, that is.

The bag was from an adult novelty shop his friend Kim owned just a little north of here. He could only make out two of the items in the bag but they were enough to send his blood pressure skyrocketing—the first was what looked to be the tiniest pair of sheer white panties that would effectively cover nothing and, Lord help him, a silver bullet vibrator.

He was going to have a stroke.

Stifling a groan over how the word 'stroke' instantly made him think about rubbing one off, he gripped the edge of the dresser like a man possessed.

The door was just a few feet away.

He could make it.

But first he needed to get some much needed air into his lungs.

Breathe, you moron!

He dragged in a breath.

And that's when he heard it.

The tiniest whisper of a giggle.

"Why you little—" Connor lunged at Abby as she shrieked out in laughter and tried ducking around him to make for the door. Snatching her around the waist, he hoisted her cackling body up over his shoulder and tossed her back onto the bed. "You set me up."

Her giggles effervesced, the unliddable glee in her eyes giving zero credence to all her perfectly scandalized denials.

He trapped her under him, burying his grin against the curve of her neck, reveling in the unfamiliar experience of having fun with a woman in bed without sex being a factor. As he skimmed a smile over her collarbone, he felt the gasp she couldn't contain like a shot of spiked adrenaline racing through his veins.

Heading straight for his heart.

It took more effort than usual to block its path.

The surprising discovery simply gave his lips even more purpose when they sought out her soft skin once again. Nothing could distract his brain from overthinking things more effectively than that; she was better than scotch in her brain-muddling effects. "You planted that wicked little bag-o-fun there for me to find. Admit it."

The woman could've won an Oscar for the gasp she flung back his way. "*What?* Now why would I go and do something like that?"

Connor tamped down his urge to laugh and nipped at her earlobe instead. "To drive me up the wall? Send me bursting through my zipper?" A satisfied grin broke through on its own accord. "Though I guess I should be flattered to be the reason you bought all that stuff."

The cutest derisive snort he'd ever heard shot out of her then—like an impeccably aimed torpedo. "Late breaking news, Connor: scientists have in fact discovered that the earth doesn't revolve around you; women buy toys for themselves all the time."

He grit his teeth and did everything short of reciting

tort law to avoid even *thinking* about Abby having any sort of toy-based fun.

Sitting up, he declared sternly, "Foul."

"What? On what grounds?" Her obvious war between indignation and amusement wasn't lost on him. Damn, he was having fun.

"When I agreed to your little who-can-resist-who stint, you didn't say anything about weaponizing our attacks."

She blinked innocently. "Weapons? You make them sound so sinister. I'd say they're more like…private tools. Survival tools, if you will. For my time here. Naturally, you were never meant to see them."

"*Bull.* Next, you'll tell me the snowflake masquerading as underwear in that bag is worn strictly for comfort. Hell, I've seen more fabric on the teeny doilies in Skylar's toy tea sets—"

"Ohhh," she cut in softly with a smile. "I remember those. Whenever I'd babysit, she always used to go on and on about how her 'bestest Uncle Connor' hosted the fanciest dress-up tea parties."

"I wore suits," he clarified gruffly, "and don't change the subject. Why buy sexy lingerie if not to have them be seen?"

By me.

He didn't have to say it out loud, they were both thinking it.

And his ego was celebrating it.

Abby's chin lifted stubbornly. "What do you mean, why? Easy access, of course," she answered, straight-faced. "You know what they say…better felt than seen."

His imagination went nuts.

Picturing Abby wearing the microscopic scrap of lace he saw earlier for easy access *in private* unhinged him, propelled him to shackle her wrists above her head with one hand and begin tickling her ribs with the other. "Another foul."

"Stop!" she screeched, dissolving into a breathless puddle of mirth. "Okay, I admit it! These were all dirty, dirty fouls on my part; you should definitely take a free throw shot."

He paused, wondering where she was going with this.

She pointed to the trashcan. "There's the basket. My new panties can be the ball…since yours are clearly in a twist."

Incredulous, he dialed up the tickle torture to merciless.

Her squealing 'I-take-it-backs' hit an ultrasonic range as she wriggled and squirmed and bucked until soon, he was fairly certain he was suffering more than she was.

Breathing hard, he released her wrists and rolled onto his back beside her. "You're planning to drive me completely crazy these next few weeks, aren't you?"

Dangling half off the bed, limbs all akimbo, she heaved between breaths, "Like you wouldn't believe."

With a groaning chuckle, he dragged her up to steal a long, hard kiss while she was too tickle-drunk to object. And the smile he couldn't seem to contain around her snuck up on him once again.

Mostly because she'd sobered up enough to proclaim weakly, "Foul…and a really mean one at that."

For the first time in his life, two weeks of imposed abstinence didn't seem all that bad.

CHAPTER NINE

⁓

IT WAS WORSE THAN BAD.

It was impossible. Six days of pure, unmitigated, using-up-all-the-cold-water agony. And there were still eight days ahead to face.

Survival was looking highly unlikely.

He had to admit though that the last six days had been pretty great in their own right.

Fun.

Given the constraints of her busy writing schedule, Connor made sure to limit himself to only one short, concentrated flirt session with Abby a day, either by phone or a flurry of text message bantering.

And every night, she'd greet him at home with a radiant smile, and depending on how steamy their flirting had been that day, a damn cute blush, too.

It was addictive.

After seeing her warming his home her first night there, he'd found it impossible to stay away each following night as well. Sure, he still had his occasional evening meetings and late office work but he always made sure to be 'home by dinner.'

What a concept.

Growing up, his father had never felt a need to do it more than once, maybe twice a week. Even though he'd had a wife and two sons waiting at home for him. As a kid, Connor had missed him, from middle school on, not so much. Now as an adult with someone to actually come home to for once—regardless how temporary it was—he felt renewed disappointment in his father. Again.

Or rather, still.

"I cooked us up some Greek food tonight," called out a cheerful voice from the kitchen, breaking into his thoughts, luring him over to where all the sumptuous smells were originating.

The sight of Abby bent over pulling something out from the oven was the best thing he'd set his eyes on all day...at least until she plopped the baking tin on the stove and gifted him with her most dazzling, room-brightening smile yet.

Then *that* officially became the greatest thing he'd seen all day.

Perhaps all year.

Yeah, it took a real bastard not to want to come home to this every night.

"Hi honey, I'm home." He just wanted to try it on for size. Strangely, it felt good. Like a vintage suit tailored just for him. Tomorrow, maybe he'd even go pre-technicolor and trip over an ottoman on his way in. Milk the novelty of this all while it lasted.

"Everything looks great." He kissed her cheek—the only body part she was letting him kiss. For now. "But you should've told me you were making such specific dishes; I would've ordered the groceries you needed online and had them delivered."

"Don't be silly. You've been paying for groceries more than I have as it is, which makes zero sense," she retorted. "Plus, this whole culinary traveling around the world adventure is my thing. You shouldn't have to pay for it."

"I'm eating it," he argued back.

"Just like I've eaten on the nights you've cooked." She gave him a look that said, 'so there.'

See now if the lawyers he faced in court looked half that cute during their rebuttals, he was sure he'd lose a whole lot more.

Grinning, he conceded, "Okay then. Since tomorrow's my turn to cook, what say I jump on this tour of yours and whip up something really exotic. Like mac & cheese with weenies."

Abby giggled. "What is it with you and all these

comfort Americana dishes? Looking at you, I'd never picture it. Were you one of those that cooked with your mom growing up?"

He snorted. "Hardly. We had a cook, which freed up mother to drink her three square meals more often than not."

"Oh." A regretful frown dimmed her face. "I'm sorry I brought it up."

"Hey." He tipped her chin up. "No feeling bad over the poor little rich kid with the present-but-still-absent parents. Did I mention I had my own pony growing up? Well, it was on lease at the polo club but still, how many kids can say that?"

The stubborn glaze of tears in her eyes unnerved him.

No one ever cried for him. Because of him, yes— more than he cared to think about—but never *for* him.

He bent down and fit his mouth to hers, telling himself it was just a comfort kiss. To take away some of her sadness. Inside, he knew he was really just capturing the memory for himself so he could open it like a Christmas gift one day when she was long gone.

God, when was the last time he'd actually gotten a gift? Wrapped personally just for him?

Years, maybe.

Suddenly, the parched thirst for every desire he'd been denied this past week, every variety of warmth and affection he hadn't really ever noticed not having until now had him pouring his soul into their kiss like a lost man aching to be found.

Soon, comfort was the last thing on his mind.

"You're killing me here," he drew back, but not far. Brushing his lips against her soft lips back and forth, he was amazed at how alive the simple contact felt, how every last little experience was more vibrant with Abby. "I don't think I can last another week of this. Wanting you this bad without having you."

Her breathless, "Me neither," did nothing to cool him down. Without another thought, he lifted her onto the granite and slid between her legs, feeling her heat even through the cotton barrier of her shorts.

"Good lord, you're huge," she gasped.

He'd have smiled if he weren't gritting his teeth hard enough to crack a molar. "And you're wet. For me." He traced his tongue over the racing pulse at her throat, the beat a near match to the pounding he felt all through his veins. "If you really want to stop, tell me now."

It'd be pure torture, but he'd back off if she said the word.

Before she could say anything at all, however, he thrust his hips against hers again in reminder—and promise—of what a 'yes' would entail.

A rush of male satisfaction assailed him when she moaned and locked her legs around his waist. He knew he wasn't playing fair, but right now, it was hard to police himself. Not with her teeth raking across his neck every time he rocked against her. Not when every gorgeous sound coming out of her just made him even harder.

Want her even more.

His name fell from her lips then and he almost lost it. Raw and needy, the sound was pure sex-on-tape. And the look on her face as she said it cast a thick, lust-filled spell on him. Had him growling in hunger by the time she finally pulled him in for a kiss—the first one he hadn't had to instigate between them since she'd moved in.

Christ, it was sweet.

With hands unsteady with lust, his fingers sank into her lush curves, sealing her tight against him as he pushed harder against her core. Every quick, broken cry she couldn't hold in was like a blazing hot homing beacon, steering him as he nudged his erection higher, slipping over the one spot that effectively scattered her voice, hijacked her breathing, and compelled her to all but ride him as he did his best to simply hold on and take stock of what little control he had left.

"Touch me," she whispered.

His restraint snapped.

He slid a hand under the hem of her t-shirt, undid her bra and pushed the offensive thing out of his way. Skimming her shirt up slowly, his lips soon broke away from hers on a groan.

Plump and ripe, she filled his hand and then some. She was perfection. Softly rounded and feminine, just like the rest of her. Delicate. *Sexy*.

He had to taste her.

"No, wait." It came out as a raw, almost inaudible whimper. "Stop."

For one horrifying moment, he truly thought he wouldn't be able to.

Jaw clenched, eyes shut tight, he forced in an unsteady breath and somehow managed to inch back at the very last second with a ragged curse that blew hot and harsh across her pale pink skin.

She cried out. The sensation making her arch and send her taut nipple grazing against lips.

He wasn't strong enough.

A better man could've fought the temptation but not him. Not now. Not when it came to Abby. Groaning, he lashed his tongue out and dragged it over the sensitive peak awaiting him. Once. Twice.

She asked you to stop.

He yanked himself back, panting, appalled at his lack of restraint, appalled that even amidst his self-flogging, his mind was still a tornado of images all locked on him taking her right there on the counter, over and over until stopping was the last thing either of them would be capable of. Until they burned through whatever this was building between them.

And then instantly started all over again.

Holy shit. He curled his hands into fists and kept his eyes off her naked breasts, away from everything he couldn't have, so goddamn close he could taste it.

Did taste it…for three mind-bending seconds.

"I…" she began, crossing an arm over her chest.

"No need to explain," he cut in, voice strained. "I told you to tell me if you wanted to stop." He shoved his hands into his pockets, trying like hell to punch out some space for his raging hard-on. "I better go up and get changed for dinner."

A tiny, trembling hand on his arm prevented his escape. "I'm so sorry, Connor. I'm not trying to be a tease or anything, I swear. I just need to stick to something when I say I will. Especially *this* something."

"Forget about it," his voice gentled. "Don't apologize for saying no, Abby. You can always, always say no."

Her hand fell away. And something in her silence made him study her face closely. "Honey? Are you okay?"

"That's just it. Just because I *can* doesn't mean I always did. Which is why I need to stick to these two weeks." She shook her head sadly. "You wouldn't understand."

No, he was starting to get that he didn't understand anything fully when it came to Abby, when it came to what was clearly more than just the game of wits and stamina he'd thought it to be.

"Then why don't you explain it to me, sweetheart."

CHAPTER TEN

"IT'S ALL YOUR FAULT, you know," she teased with a rueful shrug, trying to make light of the situation, knowing that she now had Connor's undivided attention. "I've never had a problem sticking to my guns until now. That's why I made that stupid wager with you. Because I got cocky with an undefeated record that's spanned over thirteen years."

Abby gazed at him, at the concern she saw etched in his beautiful features. For years now, she'd watched him from afar, always knowing whenever he was really concerned about something because his eyes would go from its normally intense pale blue to the softest gray, usually when he was looking at Beth and Brian.

She'd never, ever wanted those sympathetic gray

eyes aimed her way.

Too late now.

"You joke about my being a nice girl. But I wasn't always. In high school, I was the furthest thing from it."

At his disbelieving expression, she scoffed. "Believe me, it's true. 'Til my sophomore year, I was just me. Just Abby. A nothing, really...until one guy told me he saw me as something." She exhaled softly. "It was the prototypical teen dream—an older, popular, incredibly hot guy looking at me in ways no one ever had before. And he was exciting. Not because he was some rebel without a clue, either. In fact, he was actually top of the senior class and an all-star athlete to boot. Your basic high school stud, really...who had it bad for corrupting good little girls."

Feeling Connor tense, she looked away, afraid of what she'd see in his expression. "Seemed everyone but me knew how much he got off on finding the most pristine girls and turning them into playthings that would do anything he asked."

"That was me my junior year. At first, it was only a little dominant play here and there. Nothing major. Kind of fun, in fact. But then a month or so in, he started pushing me past my comfort zone more and more, but just a little at a time."

She fiddled with her pan of *spanakopita*. "I remember, actually, exactly when it was that he'd started pushing. We were hanging out with his friends one night and he asked me to flash everyone, just once, to 'show them how hot his girl was.' I didn't want to. And I'd felt so young and silly for saying no. Mostly because he'd seemed so matter-of-fact about it, so shocked when I didn't do it right away."

She shook her head at the memory. "When I looked over and saw him looking so completely disappointed by my refusal, I just...shut out that voice in my head yelling no and simply yanked up my top and bra without thinking. After his friends finished hooting and hollering, he spent the entire rest of the night treating me like a princess. And I remember distinctly feeling like what I'd done had been totally worth it."

"From then, his requests started to get more intense. In the beginning, I swear, I said no. A lot. But he'd changed his tactic from the flashing incident, going with a more sweet and cajoling approach that somehow had me starting to say no less and less each time."

Blinking slowly, she met Connor's gaze head-on, "I'm not saying this was all his fault, because it wasn't. Yes, I felt pressured by the thought of losing him but part of me felt okay going with it as long as it was under the pretense of 'him making me do it.' That became the easy button for me to push to do every depraved thing he wanted me to do."

"The first time he had me do something for a bigger crowd was at his friend's house with a bunch of his teammates after they'd just won a big game. All the other guys' girlfriends were there too. And after a few beers, most of the couples had started making out and stuff. No big deal. I was doing the same with my boyfriend. But somewhere along the line, it was like I blinked and a full-blown game of musical chairs with sex partners was suddenly happening all around me. Then out of the blue, I was picked up off the couch and led down on to my knees by these two massive linebackers."

"That's when he came to my rescue. My boyfriend. He pulled me off to the side and told me how he didn't want to share me with any of his friends. I was so damn *thankful* for that, for him. So when he went on to explain that I could I just give him a blowjob in front of everyone to get them off my back, I did it. Without any hesitation."

She swallowed the acrid taste in her mouth at the vivid memory. "Can you believe I'd felt *special* that night? To be the one girl whose guy wouldn't share her." She laughed bitterly at herself. "Of course, it was just all part of his long con."

"After that night, for a while, everything was great. Fairytale-like. I was so smitten with him that a part of me did this whole 'told-you-it-wasn't-a-big-deal' thing. Which is probably why I was so blindsided by the party at his friend's house a few weeks later—basically a huge orgy."

Abby watched the muscle tick in Connor's cheek and did her best to tamp down her mortification. "He said the same thing as last time, that all I'd have to do was 'perform,' no big deal. But then before I knew what was happening, all my clothes were dragged off by what felt like a hundred hands and he'd kissed me up onto the center of the dining table with everyone surrounding it, guys and girls. And video cameras."

She didn't realize she was shaking until she felt Connor squeeze her hand. "I still remember the big crystal chandelier above that dining table. Weird, huh? There I was naked in front of dozens of kids, half of whom didn't even go to my school, and all I could do was stare at that chandelier. Half hoping it would fall from the ceiling so I could stop. Get up and go home. But it didn't fall. It kept right on hanging there, twinkling at me…"

"…While I masturbated for them all."

Something dark and vicious crossed Connor's face.

Along with pity.

Stifling, drowning shame almost prevented her from going on. But she continued, wanting, needing him to understand. "I can still hear them yelling, egging me on. But I just couldn't…finish. So they started demanding I do other things instead with the other girls and guys there. I was drunk, and a little high off pot, but I still knew for certain that I didn't want to. I'd had more than enough."

Though she'd replayed that night hundreds of times in her head, the next part still slammed her like a wrecking ball each time. "When I started crying and grabbing my clothes to leave, my boyfriend just wrapped his arms around me and began 'comforting' me. Telling me how he'd never been more turned on in his life watching me up there. He laid it on thick, telling me how unbelievably sexy I was, how special I was to him. And then he busted out the big guns. He looked me square in the eye and told me he loved me. *Loved me*. That's all it took. Three little words and I was crawling back on that table, holding his proud gaze while I headed over to the small group of kids who'd taken my place in the spotlight. All the while, the cheering from around the table got so loud…"

She shut her eyes. "It was so loud I didn't hear my parents come barging into the room."

Knife-sharp humiliation and remorse sliced through her fresh like it did every time she saw their devastated faces in her mind.

Connor's face right now was just as cutting.

"Apparently, some girl from the party had called my house, told my parents where I was and that I was in trouble. I never found out who though. I never got to thank her for putting a halt to something I would've regretted more than having my folks see me like that—as the free entertainment at a high school sex party."

She trudged through the rest, didn't bother glossing over how stupid she'd really been back then. "My parents didn't say a word. They just threw a jacket on me and rushed me out to their car so fast, I almost didn't see my boyfriend in all the chaos. But he made sure I did. He planted himself next to the entrance and blew me a kiss goodbye…before turning to a drunk girl beside him and pulling off her top. Her skirt came off next. And then he started feeling her up right there in front of me. Showing me how quickly he could replace me. Watching and smirking at me the whole time. And I actually cried over that, over *him* the entire ride home."

"I would've killed him," Connor snarled then, enraged. "Still could if you give me his name. That guy was a sick, twisted psycho who took advantage of you, Abby. He broke you, practically brainwashed you. For chrissakes, you were what, only seventeen?"

"Sixteen. And yeah, that's what my folks kept telling me." Hot tears welled in her eyes. "To this day, I still can't believe I put them through all that." Her voice broke. "After how hard they worked to give me a great childhood, that's how I repaid them. I didn't have a sad home life or tragic backstory; my own selfish idiocy was the sole reason I'd turned into a teenage slut."

"*Don't ever call yourself that!*"

She jumped, never having heard such a hard edge to his voice before. "But I was. For him, at least. It's okay. I don't blame myself or anything self-destructive like that. I certainly don't absolve him or think of him as anything less than a sociopathic piece of scum who deserves every karmic torture coming his way in hell. But I don't ignore or make excuses for my part in it either. I'm not proud of who I was then and my not sweeping it under a rug is what has made me who I am today. Like you said, I could've said no at any point. It was on me that I didn't."

When he started to object, she shook her head

firmly. "No. Don't try to convince me otherwise. I was a victim, yes, but a participant as well. My body, my decisions. And as you can see," she waved her hands over herself. "I turned out just fine. From porn star to professor."

"That's not funny," he bit out.

"Yeah, my mom doesn't like that joke either. Whenever I make a crack like that she always scolds me and tells me I should let go of the past. Let go more, period. She seems to think I overcorrected a bit with my life, but I don't. I like who I am now. If guys call me a goodie-goodie stuck-up tease, so be it. I know who I am."

"And who is that, Abby?" asked Connor softly.

"I'm the nice girl by choice—my wish, my reality."

His eyes hardened. "So now I'm the new asshole corrupting that reality."

Her brows shot up in alarm. "What?! No!"

"Is that what the sexual inquisition was about the other day?" Now he sounded downright livid. "All that threesome talk? Is that what you think of me? You think I'm like that *monster* who tortured you in high school?!"

"Of course not!" she gasped. "I asked you all that because I was genuinely curious. Honestly, what happened when I was sixteen had less to do with the sex and more to do with the control. The control I gave up over my own life."

When he looked unconvinced, she grabbed his wrist. "I'm telling you the truth."

"Are you?" He pulled away. "You tell me guys basically call you frigid but here you were the other day asking me about every raunchy thing I've ever done. I know you weren't just teasing me, either; you're just not built like that. So what the hell, Abby? Do you see me the way you saw that guy? Do you feel like you have to turn into a slutty plaything for me? Because it's not true; not at all. I'd hate to have any woman be like that for me."

"I know that, Connor, I swear. I wasn't planning on losing myself with you, or *for* you. All that talk wasn't specific to you. I'd have had the same questions for any guy whose sexual history differed from mine. In fact, I make sure of it so we both know what we're getting into. I'm not repeating the mistakes I made back then; I know the difference between identity and fantasy now. Whether or not I like your fantasies, I'm not changing my identity. Not for you or for any man."

"Stop talking about being with another man!" he exploded.

She eyed him warily.

"What if I'd wanted the threesomes, Abby? What then?"

"I-I would've considered it seriously...and decided if it was something I really wanted."

"So consider it now. Humor me." His scowl was fierce.

She shoved a ruthless lid on her embarrassment, trying desperately to show she really did want a logical discussion about this. Heck, she'd had it with each of the three other guys she'd dated seriously in the past. Just…in a far more hypothetical manner, since their fantasy sexcapades didn't come close to Connor's real life history. "I'd be too jealous to share you with another woman," she confessed. "So I'd have said no to that right off the bat."

A low grunt was his only response.

"As for you and another guy." She bit her lip. "I admit the thought of it is a little hot. But…" How was she supposed to explain it? How was she supposed to tell him that she wouldn't, couldn't even remotely consider a threesome if true emotions were involved…something that was fast becoming the case with Connor. "I feel like I'd lose the connection of being with you, just the two of us. So no, I wouldn't want that either."

He gave her a measured look before replying gruffly, "I feel the same way."

She smiled at his clipped, audibly relieved response. There, that wasn't so bad. "Then it's settled—no threesomes. See? Mature and rational. I know when I brought it up the other day we were goofing around but this was what I wanted. This control right here? I *gave* him this when I was sixteen. That's what I hated the most about it all. So now I keep that control secured tight. Live by it, rise and fall by it."

His expression softened. "That's what you meant when you said you *need* the two weeks you asked for? For control?"

"Yes. Back then, I felt like I didn't know my own mind, and that the few times I did, I didn't stand up for what I wanted, good or bad. If I'd wanted to be a slut, I wouldn't have hated myself so much. But that wasn't the case. I was weak, every bit the mindless plaything he'd turned me into. Too scared to admit to him what I did and didn't want, and foolish enough to convince myself that his wants were mine."

She unloaded a long, emotional breath as she reflected on all these tenets of her life that she hadn't thought about in awhile. "I'm never going back to that. Not in any shape or form. Now, every decision in my life is mine. I take a good look at my wishes, whatever they may be, and work hard to make them my reality. That's how I came back from all of it, by taking 100% ownership of my life."

She slid a hand along his cheek. "And that's what I'm realizing I should've been doing here all along. With us. This past week, I haven't been totally honest with myself on what I truly want. I hid from it. From you. The truth is, you are most definitely a wish I want to become my reality. Even if it's only going to be a short reality."

That last part made him flinch.

"I'm entering this with my eyes wide open," she reassured him. "Telling you my sordid past simply reminded me how being scared to admit to and hold true to what I really want never got me anywhere good. You're what I want, Connor. What I've wanted for a while if I'm being perfectly honest."

She felt his heart rate pick up under her palm.

"Dammit, Abby. You can't offer yourself up to me on a silver platter after telling me everything you just did."

"I know. So that's why we should just do what we had planned. Eat, talk, and watch a movie. For tonight."

"And tomorrow?"

"I'll be just like your other one-month women." She smothered her body's immediate objection to that statement and held his gaze. "I'm not resisting what I want anymore."

The latter half, her body didn't have any complaints over, seeing as how it was the absolute truth.

Resisting Connor Sullivan was no longer an option.

CHAPTER ELEVEN

⚬⚬⚬

As far as morning after big declarations go, Abby decided this one was going fairly smoothly.

Probably because they were both on their laptops pretending they weren't sitting six feet from each other.

Around the third mumbled apology when their hands collided reaching for something on the table, however, was when she started getting pissed.

Shoot, if she only had another three weeks with the man, this was *not* how she was going to spend it.

She grabbed her phone and started texting.

>> *WERE THE WHITE PANTIES THE ONLY ONE YOU SAW?*

>> *...YOU KNOW, THAT DAY IN MY LIL' BAG-O-FUN?*

She kept her eyes down as Connor reached for his beeping phone.

A tiny flash of amusement flickered over his features, soon followed by a hint of wariness. Good. She liked him off-kilter.

Seconds later, he was texting back. Four quick taps.

>> *YES.*

Pause.

>> *WHY?*

She smiled, waiting far longer than she needed to reply.

>> *BECAUSE I BOUGHT A PAIR OF RED ONES, TOO.*

Another pause. And just the slightest gulp.

>> *THAT'S...INTERESTING. GOOD FOR YOU.*

That's it? Eyes narrowed, she kicked it up a notch.

>> *THX. I LIKE EM. MOSTLY BECAUSE THEY'RE, WELL...*

She dragged it out. This was too much fun.

>> *LESS 'CONSERVATIVE' THAN THE WHITE PAIR.*

A choked throat clearing sputtered out from his end of the dining room.

Excellent.

>> *PLUS, IT'S NOT 'EASY ACCESS,' BUT RATHER...*

She tapped the second half of the text out, but purposely didn't put it through. Out of the corner of her eye, she saw Connor practically glaring at his phone.

He broke first.

>> *RATHER, WHAT?*

She clicked send.

>> *ALL ACCESS.*

"Jesus Christ."

It was a hiss more than anything else and oh, so delicious. Now to go in for the kill…

"I'm wearing them now." She said it aloud instead of texting it. And saw instant, white-hot desire flare up in his eyes.

An answering rush of heat charged through her.

"Abby, we don't have to do this." The corners of his mouth softened into a look of genuine affection as he studied her from across the table. "I was wrong. We can most definitely be friends. I've really enjoyed this past week with you. More than I'd ever imagined possible."

"But—"

"No, just listen. You're special to me, Abby. I hated hearing you say you were going to be just like my other one-month women." He held her gaze. "You'll never be 'just' anything. Let alone that."

Emotions swelled up out of her chest. Every day in every way Connor just kept getting more irresistible. "You promised me the one month, Connor. I want it."

The look in his eyes switched from desire to determination as he walked over to her and held out his hand. "Come outside with me for a bit."

Abby looked at him like he'd lost his mind. "What? Now?"

"Please. I want to show you something."

Curiosity overruling her stubbornness, Abby took his outstretched hand and followed him out to the garage. But when he led her over to the second garage door, not the one where he parked his Lexus, she hesitated. "You're not going to show me some sex dungeon or something in there are you?"

He chuckled. "No. Nothing like that."

Feeling a buzz of excitement unfurl in her stomach over the unfamiliar, almost childlike joy she saw in his eyes, she turned quickly to see what was behind the mystery door, the slow hum of the rising garage door motor resounding like a drumroll.

"You're kidding me."

Beaming proudly, he circled the gunpowder black car, trailing his hand along the hood. "It's a 1971 Dodge Charger."

Looking at its iconic design, she asked the first thing that popped in her mind. "Like the *Dukes of Hazzard* car?"

Another chuckle. "Similar. That was a '69. This one was the first of the third generation Chargers. A class of its own." He took another lap around the car before patting the top of it as if to say, 'good boy.'

She realized she was still gaping a bit but seeing Connor petting and talking so affectionately about this gritty muscle car was making her brain do cartwheels.

"Do you like it?"

The question came out casually, but she could hear the current of emotion filtering around it. This was important to him. A test of sorts. Realizing this, she took a step back and gave his car an honest look.

Along with a classic, streamlined shape, the car had

one of those rugged vented hoods—not quite *Fast and the Furious* but close. It had character. Quietly powerful. Nostalgically masculine. And sexy as hell with Connor leaning against it.

Taking a deep breath, she ventured, "Actually, I do like it. I mean I don't know a lot about cars but I do have memories of my dad and uncle working on this sixties convertible on the weekends when I was a kid. Clearly, they were really bad at it because it was still barely running when they 'finished' a few years later. But I remember playing inside it a lot while they were tinkering with the engine."

She smiled and peeked at the interior. "This car reminds me of that one. And though I can't explain why, it sort of reminds me of you, too."

She must've answered right, because he rewarded her with a slow smile so luminous, she froze and simply watched it play across his face. Afraid any sudden movements would scare it away.

"I wasn't nearly as ambitious as your dad and uncle. I had this professionally restored."

The way his voice changed, warmed when he talked about the car, made an emotional lump grow in her throat. She'd never heard him speak this way about anyone or anything until now. This was a glimpse at a side of Connor she knew very few—if any—got to see.

"Tell me about your car, Connor." Her voice sounded hoarse to her own ears.

"It's a pretty recent purchase. I got it a few months ago when I made equity partner."

"Interesting midlife car choice," she teased gently.

He barked out a laugh. "See, this is why you could never be 'just' one my other women. Not one of them would ever call me old. At least not until after I'd ended things with them."

"Just imagine what things I'll say when things are over between us," she joshed lightly. She'd meant it as a joke but immediately regretted it when some of the light left Connor's eyes. "Hey, I was kidding."

Instead of responding, he asked simply, "You want to go for a ride?"

Desperately wanting to repair things, she tried again for humor, "Can I drive?"

Thankfully, his smile returned. "On the way back, I promise."

Before he could head over to the driver's side, however, she caught his arm. "I'm sorry for what I said."

"Don't be." He looked into her eyes and said softly, "It wasn't what you said; it was the reminder that our days are numbered. I get sad thinking about it is all."

That right there was the exact moment Abby knew...she wasn't in danger of just getting her heart broken by Connor; she was in danger of losing it to him completely.

CHAPTER TWELVE

———— ❧ ————

A COMFORTABLY SILENT half hour later, they were headed north with the windows down and the engine rumbling loud and low.

All the while, Abby couldn't stop staring at Connor; he'd never looked so free, so happy.

So content.

By the time he pulled over on a deserted gravel road near Cactus Creek, he was a different man. Just a man. No longer a big time corporate attorney.

"No one even knows I have this car."

"Really? Why not? This is kind of a chick magnet."

Even his laughter sounded different. More alive. "Not to any of the women I usually date."

"Maybe if you showed them the interior…" she

suggested, running an appreciative hand along the wide, buttery soft seat that was specifically designed to look, but not be vintage, and also allow her to slide all the way over to Connor if she so desired.

"A woman after my own heart. The bench seats were a custom install." He flashed her a wicked grin. "Unlike the original ones, however, these do this—"

He reached on his side of the seat and she let out a yelp as the entire front bench seat reclined down flat, lining up with the back seat and in effect, turning the car into a giant bed on wheels.

She unbuckled her seatbelt and rolled over to him, laughing. "This is so awesomely cheesy. You've really never brought a woman riding in this?"

"Nope. I usually just drive it out here and take a short nap in whatever shade I can find. Some weeks, it's the most restful sleep I get."

"Because you're free." It was a statement, not a question.

He looked up at her, startled. "Is it that obvious?"

"Only because of the goofy look on your face," she said as she put her head on his chest.

His arm came around her and she closed her eyes, listened to the silence of the desert forest surrounding them.

"It's funny how you and I have lived such distinctly opposite lives. You see me as a bad boy now but growing up, I was the perfect kid. No bad habits, a 4.3 gpa, and a spot-free room you could feature in a magazine."

"And you're related to Brian how again?"

He chuckled. "I envied him when we were younger, you know. Not his messy room, of course, but his way of life. He always seemed to go through life with such ease, good at everything but never wanting for anything. All of our father's expectations for him slid right off him like a magnet on its back."

His voice warmed with brotherly admiration. "Brian was going to be what he was going to be, period."

Abby smiled. "He's still like that."

"I'm glad. Unlike my father, I never wanted Brian to lose that."

"Why do you two hate him so much?" Her eyes popped open in surprise at the brain leak. "Sorry, you don't have to answer that."

"No, it's okay. I don't know if Brian hates our father so much as disrespects him as a parent, a feeling that has multiplied infinitely since Skylar was born. *I*, on the other hand, do hate the man. I have since the fourth grade, from the day I saw him sucking face with some woman who wasn't my mother, and then coming home to make her feel small for no reason at all later that night."

A hard edge darkened his expression. "Before that day, I used to work really hard in school to try and gain his approval, to get him to just stop and notice me. For once in my life. But he never did. Brian, my mother, and I simply didn't register on his radar. We were merely an obligation. If even that. The only thing he cared about was his work, and all those other women he was screwing around with."

Abby couldn't imagine anyone being so callous to their own family.

Connor shrugged. "After the fourth grade, I kept on getting good grades, but for myself, not for him anymore. Then by the time I was in high school, my motivation to do well academically shifted to one goal: going away to a school on the east coast without having to ask my father for a penny."

"Hence, Columbia."

"Yep. And since I wasn't the athlete Brian was, I had to rely solely on academics to get me a scholarship. Ironically, that was the one and only time I ever remember my father sounding even remotely proud of me. The day I found out that I'd gotten my full ride there."

"That must've felt good."

"You'd think." His jaw muscle ticked. "But then he ruined it by immediately mapping out my whole life for me—law school at Stanford and eventually a partnership in his firm so I could be the second Sullivan listed on the door. As always, it was still all about him. I know it sounds petty but I remember practically *gloating* when I stopped him and told him there was no chance in hell I was majoring in pre-law or going to law school. Hell, I almost fell over in shock when I saw him actually display an emotion then. A little one of annoyance. Of course, ten seconds later, he just dismissed me completely once again, shoved me back to the completely invisible status I shared with my mother and brother."

Abby listened to Connor practically spit the words out, utter them with such hostile contempt that she was momentarily too thrown to ask how in the world his life ended up taking the very road he'd swore it never would—Stanford Law and the youngest senior partner at Caldwell, Sullivan & Phillips.

Then she did the math.

He was three years older than Brian; he'd been a senior at Columbia when Brian found out Beth was pregnant. Of course. "You went to law school for Brian," she said quietly.

He stiffened.

She pulled back and looked at his shuttered eyes. "Does Brian know?"

"No, and you can't tell him. He thinks I always wanted to go to law school."

She remained silent, giving him the chance to get it all out. Undoubtedly for the first time ever.

"Brian was planning on quitting college to go work full-time and build up some savings before the baby came. I couldn't let him do that. Unlike me, he'd always known what he wanted to do. My major was basically 'anything but law' while his had always been business. Honestly, Brian has a natural knack for business that in many ways surpasses mine. If he'd been the one to get a dual JD/MBA from Stanford, he'd probably be a major CEO by now."

Very true.

"But that wasn't what he wanted. He wanted to be a dad, deemed nothing more important than that from the very second that stick turned blue. So we sat together and discussed his future, weighed his options. Since teaching was another thing he'd always been interested in, he decided to apply for the teaching program at ASU and major in business and economics. A perfect life choice for him, really."

So how did Connor's going to law school fit in all this?

"The biggest obstacle Brian faced was money," he explained as if reading her mind. "When he told my parents about the pregnancy, my mother simply drank herself into oblivion as she always did, and took her usual pretend-it-wasn't-happening method of handling it to save face at the club. My father, however, was much more direct. He offered to pay for a one-way trip for Brian and Beth to go live in a different state. As if his son becoming a father as a freshman in college was the most shameful thing for *him*, the great Marcus Sullivan. After that, Brian refused not just my father's insulting offer but his tuition money as well."

Abby didn't blame him.

"So, I made a decision. I cashed out my entire savings, along with the trust fund from my grandfather that I'd just gotten control over after turning twenty-one, and bought Brian a house. I told him it was a property investment that I wanted him to live in and take care of for me while I was away. Simple enough and pretty much true. But that still left the issue of Brian's tuition. I was tapped out at that point and Brian didn't have much of a savings to speak of to cover schooling on top of day to day living. And with a baby on the way, I didn't want them to be buried in student loans when he had a perfectly good trust fund just like mine to cover his tuition and incidentals. So, I went to my father and asked him to invoke his power as trustee to release the funds to my brother even though it was three years premature."

He glowered. "My father, of course, refused. Held it hostage."

"Until you made a deal with him," Abby guessed. God, their father was a bastard.

"Yep. The agreement was that I'd follow through with all the plans he set forth for my future in exchange for that one piece of paper."

She couldn't believe it. Connor basically bargained away his entire life for his brother. For her best friend.

Voice thick with emotion, she whispered, "You're incredible, you know that right?"

A wary cloud passed over his expression. "Abby, I told you not to do that. Don't build me up to be someone I'm not."

Tears prickled in her eyes. Why couldn't he see how wonderful he was?

Frowning, he stroked her cheek. "Stop, honey. Don't cry over—"

Not wanting to hear him dismiss his actions or himself yet again, she stubbornly fused her mouth over his and just let go, allowed herself to sink into a kiss that held everything she was feeling but wouldn't dare say, everything she knew to be true about him that he simply wouldn't accept.

Emotions tangled, soul ripped bare, she started taking as much as she gave until eventually, he was kissing her back just as desperately. Threading his hands through her hair, and transforming this all into so much more than just a kiss.

Gasping, she sat back.

When had she ended up on his lap?

No matter. It was one less step for her to take. She flung off her shirt and reached for the hem of his. Skin and heat, and muscles that were tensing just from the touch of her fingers—she needed to feel it all. Now.

Two large hands trapped hers and held her tight against his stomach, stopped her from dragging his shirt open, from sliding her hands any higher over the rock-hard muscles of his abs.

So she moved lower instead.

"*Christ, Abby. Not like this.*"

The sexy gravel of his voice was so much grittier than usual. Hotter. So sexually charged she felt she'd go insane if he didn't do something, anything to quench this fire building inside her.

She could hardly make out what he was saying.

All she knew was that the mere sound of her name had never brought her this far this fast before.

It would take just one touch, just one, for her to go up in flames.

That's when it occurred to her that she couldn't open her hands. Couldn't budge them at all. Eyes closed, mind half gone, mouth still being *devoured* by his, she finally realized he was restraining her, preventing her from undoing his belt buckle.

And she lost it.

She tore her mouth from his and struggled to pull her hands free. Right now, nothing mattered more than feeling him against her. In her.

He held firm.

Frantic now, she twisted, tugged, jerked her body up against his arms, effectively bringing his knuckles right over her sensitized core. Once by accident, the second with a vengeance.

She bucked against his closed fist and fastened her lips back on his, tasted the possessed groan rumbling up his throat and nearly screamed when his hand finally, finally opened and turned to cup her heat.

The pace was no longer hers.

He was relentless, touching her in every way her own fingers could never measure up, taking her higher and harder.

Until his rough, *"Come for me, Abby,"* sent her shattering into a thousand jagged pieces.

———◆———

CONNOR WAS DROWNING in a pool of lust.

He didn't have much practice at being the good man but for Abby, he really wanted to try.

So he kept his hands chastely at her hips, his now painfully tattooed zipper fly firmly left closed, and his mind on anything but how she'd looked coming apart just for him.

He found he was really bad at being good.

When she eventually stirred from the mini-slumber she'd fallen into, she rubbed her cheek against his chest and said softly, "You know, I've never had sex in a car before." Her voice, which was always ultra-sexy, was now a full-blown sex kitten purr.

Not. Helping.

He managed an unintelligible, hoarse sound in his throat. Pretty damn good effort on his part, considering.

"Is that Neanderthal for you haven't either, or you have loads of times?" She kissed her way up his neck and whispered in his ear, "Because if you haven't, I really want to show you why my red panties aren't as conservative as my white ones."

"I haven't," he rasped, so hard now he was in serious danger of passing out from lack of blood in his brain.

She smiled against his skin and tucked a little square packet in his hand before rolling over to the middle of the seat. "Have I mentioned how much I love these seats?"

He was back to speaking Neanderthal again.

Because while he'd always loved this car, especially the interior he'd had custom restored, the sight of Abby in nothing but her red lace underwear on the creamy leather seats made his appreciation of the car reach new more reverent heights.

Wow.

"You are so beautiful."

"So are you. I've always thought so."

The way she looked at him, hell, he'd imagined nothing could get him to calm down at that point, but that look did. Because it reminded him he wanted to do this right, take it slow, cherish her.

Then she showed him the nifty 'all access' feature of her underwear...

Aaand, he was back.

In two seconds flat, condom in place, he was trying out that red lacy feature, inch by slow inch.

Holy hell. He had to shut his eyes to keep from coming on the spot.

Abby whimpered and arched and basically did everything possible to make that first gliding stroke completely mind-altering. Hot, wet, and so tight he had to stop for a second to get his bearings; she was all that he'd imagined and more.

The more being when she took control and slid him to the hilt on her own.

He'd expected nothing less.

And he would've smiled over it if he weren't so busy trying not to come.

Teeth clenched, body fighting his brain something fierce, he started a steady rhythm, a *torturous* rhythm. He dragged her hands above her, pinned them against the leather seats, and her tight, slick walls began pulsing around him in response.

Pumping into her harder, faster he buried himself as deep as he could go. Again and again. His breathing rasped against her neck, "Let me feel it again. Drive me crazy, Abby. Come for me."

She did.

His mouth came down on hers hard as she gripped him in a hot, liquid explosion that sent him hurtling over the edge right after her.

———◆———

LATER, MUCH LATER, he realized he must have blacked out there for a minute. Or ten.

When he somehow managed to regain enough brain ability to shift his weight off of her, she grumbled a sleepy protest and followed him as he rolled onto his back.

Smiling, he tucked her in against his chest and did his best to ignore the fact that her sweet weight on him was making him hard again.

Around Abby, his constant arousal was a state of being.

As was this feeling of never wanting to let her go.

It had been the same way last night when she'd fallen asleep on him during the movie. Rather than carry her back to her room right away, he'd just held her and dozed off with her for a bit.

Now here he was again, ready to fall asleep with her in his arms, liking it far more than was sensible.

The realization didn't stop him from dropping a kiss onto her hair and closing his eyes.

He'd worry about letting her go later.

CHAPTER THIRTEEN

"SO WHAT NORMALLY HAPPENS at the end of the month?"

Connor sighed. These were not normal questions he usually entertained.

"I mean, it's got to be an awkward last day," pressed Abby. "What do you do? Shake hands and provide a severance package with references?"

Damn it, looks like it was cold-hearted bastard time again. "Most times, I just leave before they wake up."

Abby's jaw dropped and he could see she was officially offended on behalf of all womankind. "You don't even leave a note? An email or text message, maybe? A grocery store flower arrangement with a 'to whom it may concern' card? *Anything?*"

Well, when she put it like that.

Her brows went up a notch. "Wow, you're kind of an asshat."

He jerked back defensively. "Why? Because I refuse to draw things out and string these women along? I've had enough of the post-one-month drama to know how each one of those gestures you just listed could play out. A call or text is always way too awkward because it puts it back on her to reply. And if she does, we're right back at the start of a vicious loop. Email isn't all that much better, and actually rather insulting if you ask me. Meanwhile, leaving a note is much, much worse. If I leave a note, then it's like leaving the hope that this isn't really goodbye for good, that I want each word I've written to be analyzed with the magic relationship decoder ring for the secret hidden message."

Oh yeah, he was officially worked up. "And a *gift*? Are you serious? If I send a gift, hell, that's the same as saying I'll be back someday so don't ever forget me." He looked her square in the eye. "Why do that to them? At least if I leave without a word, they know that's it. Door closed. The end."

She was expressionless in her silence.

"Say something," he grumbled.

"You've obviously given this a lot of thought."

"I have!"

"Everything you said is probably, twistedly more true than not."

He'd yet to realign his jaw. She wasn't getting off that easily.

"I'm sorry for calling you an asshat."

Finally.

"It's clear that your logic, though warped and jaded, comes from someplace honest and kind."

Aaand, of course. "Do you have any idea how infuriating you can be?"

She beamed. "Oh c'mon, just because you win an argument doesn't mean I can't get in some good blows. What kind of fight would that be?"

Choosing to hear only the most important part of that, he puffed up his chest in satisfaction. "So you're admitting I'm right?"

Her pert little nose went up in the air. "Most certainly not. I'm saying I get why you *think* you're right."

Laughing, he kissed the tip of her nose and began arming up to go another round when the doorbell rang.

He ran over and pulled the door open to a less than welcome swirl of Chanel and platinum blonde hair.

"Hey, babe." Victoria took off her suit jacket and popped a kiss on his lips. "If I beg really prettily will you give me one of your magic foot rubs tonight? I had a killer day today."

She pulled off her designer stilettos one at a time as if they were singlehandedly responsible for all modern torture techniques. "In return, I'll massage any part of your body you want."

Connor jerked back and took a giant step away as he silently guided Victoria's attention over to Abby on the couch.

"Oops! I'm sorry, I didn't know you had company." Victoria shrugged and grabbed his shoulder to slip her stilettos back on her feet, groaning in her usual, unintentionally triple-X way.

He threw a worried glance over at Abby, knowing how bad this looked. There was no way she could possibly know that flirting was basically Victoria's first language, and that between them, propositions involving body parts never actually meant anything.

It took him a fair amount of restraint not to forcibly shove Victoria's hand off his shoulder while she was teetering on one ridiculously high heel. Partly, because he didn't want her tripping over and showing Abby why she didn't have any panty lines under that skintight suit skirt.

Not missing a thing, Victoria soon caught wind of his panic and slid a curious smile over at Abby.

Uh-oh.

"I'm Victoria, by the way," she called out, vying for the crown of world's slowest suit jacket wearer.

He should've let her fall on her ass.

"I'm Abby," came the quiet, flat reply from the living room. He shot a quick look back her way, tried to get her to meet his eyes. She wouldn't.

Victoria tilted her head to the side. "You look so familiar. Have we met?"

Connor jumped in on that one. "I highly doubt that. This is my little brother's friend. She goes to ASU; you two don't exactly run in the same circles."

Abby went stiff.

Shit, now what'd he do? He'd only been trying to help by cutting off Victoria's interrogation. But it seemed he somehow made things worse.

One perfectly arched eyebrow directly at his eye level harassed him without saying a word, told him she wasn't leaving without at least a little more of an explanation.

"Abby's staying here for a bit while the place she's renting is being renovated." He followed that up with a pointed glare that shouted, *Now LEAVE.*

But that's when Abby chose to speak up. "Yeah, thank God for good *old* Connor here. He took pity on a starving college kid and offered to let me crash here."

Ooh, this was so not good. There was no way Abby ever used 'crash' in that context before. He'd have no choice but to forgive the 'old' crack. She was clearly pissed.

Victoria, on the other hand, looked like she was ready to split a seam laughing. "I see. Well, like I said, I didn't know Connor had company so I'm sorry for barging in."

"No, don't go." Abby got up to grab her bag and keys. "I should be heading out anyway."

What? "You didn't mention you had plans tonight."

As slippery as a ghost, Abby shot right past them and

yanked open the front door before he could stop her. "A friend invited me to go clubbing so you two can have the place all to yourselves for your massage night."

"*Abby.*" It came out a feral bark. And had zero effect on her.

She ran straight to her car. "Don't worry, I have the spare key. Have fun you two. Don't wait up!"

He glowered at her retreating figure, willing her to stop all this and come back to him. When she didn't, when she actually *drove off*, he grabbed his phone and dialed her number.

Straight to voicemail. Goddamn it!

"Oh my god. You're completely gaga over a little college kid." Victoria tsked, sounding both highly entertained and slightly awed. "My, how the mighty have fallen."

Not trusting himself to say anything that wasn't four-lettered, he kept his mouth shut and held the door open for her, foot tapping impatiently.

Victoria snickered as she walked past. "I do hope she comes back, Connor. She really is *super* cute."

He slammed the front door on her.

———◆———

1:00 AM

With each passing hour, it seemed like the time on the DVR box glowed brighter and brighter.

Mocking him.

Though she hadn't been dressed for it, and she'd mentioned before that it wasn't her scene, Connor still couldn't help but wonder if Abby did in fact end up going to some hot, sweaty club. The thought made his back teeth hurt. Probably from all the clenching.

Picturing her dancing around with other men had him on edge, territorial.

At 1:01 AM, he finally picked up his phone and unclenched long enough to text her:

>> *HAVING FUN?*

His phone beeped back a half a minute later and he exhaled in relief. At least she was still talking to him.

>> *SURE. ARE YOU?*

No. He'd missed the hell out of her all night. Tonight had been anything but fun.

>> *VICTORIA LEFT RIGHT AFTER YOU DID.*

Pause.

>> *OH. SORRY IF I RUINED YOUR PLANS FOR THE EVENING.*

He let out a frustrated breath.

>> *IT'S NOT WHAT YOU THINK. I HAVEN'T SLEPT WITH HER IN YEARS.*

Her reply was instant.

>> *HOW DO YOU KNOW WHAT I THINK?*

Replaying the look in her eyes as she'd left the house, he texted back:

>> *YOU SEEMED UPSET.*

The sound of musical chirping coming from outside his room led him out to the hallway where Abby was standing at the top of the stairwell with her phone. "Damn right I was upset."

"I told you—"

"Not over you and Victoria," she snapped. "If you want to date other women, that's your prerogative. What I *am* pissed about is being reduced to a peon in the presence of two oh-so-great attorneys. Call me a relative stranger, call me the girl you're banging, I don't care—but don't ever make me out to be anything less than I am again! I've worked hard to achieve the goals in my life. I'm not some young college kid bumming on your couch. How the heck would you feel if I'd referred to you in that way during your last year of law school?"

God, she was magnificent when she was angry. "I see your point. I'm sorry." He got within arm's reach of her but kept his hands in his pockets. Barely. "If it helps, you did a good job getting me back. I've been going out of my mind wondering if you really were out dancing up on a bunch of guys while I was sitting here all alone. Jealous."

She jutted her chin out at him. "Good. Serves you right."

Taking extra measures not to touch him, she cleared a wide path around him and headed for her room. "I'm not sleeping with you tonight, Connor."

Huh, he didn't think she was the type to hold sex hostage.

When she turned back to face him, a touch of vulnerability marred her features. "I'm not being a shrew. I just...don't want to be sloppy seconds to Victoria."

"I swear I didn't lay a finger on her."

"But you still had your lips on another woman tonight. Right in front of me."

"*She* kissed me. And I backed away as soon as I could."

"It doesn't matter. I'm sure you wouldn't care about this sort of thing if the positions were reversed, but—"

"Hell, if the positions were reversed, I'd make damn sure to kiss you silly until I wiped every last trace of any other man's kiss from your memory completely," he growled.

That familiar Abby light returned to her eyes. "I can see how that'd be...ah, effective."

Seeing her gaze travel down to his lips and then shoot back up again, he took a cautious step forward, teasing lightly, "Want to try that tactic with me?"

She crossed her arms over her chest. "You don't reward the puppy that misbehaves. It tends to confuse the poor thing."

He chuckled and pulled her into his arms. "God, I missed you tonight." He brought her close and breathed in the sweet scent of her hair. She always smelled so good. "You didn't go clubbing tonight, did you?"

"No. I didn't feel like it. So, I went to the library instead and then met up with a friend for coffee."

He none-so-subtly corralled her back to his room. "A male friend?"

"Her name's Megan."

"Glad to hear it," he said gruffly. Gazing at her in his arms, outlined by the moonlight, he could still see the lingering traces of hurt in her eyes. "I'm sorry your feelings were hurt today."

Brushing a light kiss on her lips, he asked, "If I promise not to ravage you, will you at least come to bed with me? I find I sleep...better with you here."

It was true. With her tucked in his arms, perfectly fitted against him, he experienced a bone-deep comfort he'd never had before in his life.

After studying him carefully for a beat, she nodded and headed for the other side of the bed. "Fair warning though, I have to get up really early in the morning to meet with some teachers at one of my research schools on res. It's my first and only chance to talk with them all together at once."

"I'm sorry, could you repeat that? What I think I heard you say was that it's a *good thing* you stayed here instead of going back to California."

She smothered a grin and volleyed back, "So about that kiss..."

Ouch. "Early in the morning, research on the reservation. Got it. So I guess we better hit the hay."

Her chuckling smile turned into a wary look as she watched him climb under the covers. "You swear you'll keep your hands to yourself tonight?"

"Scout's honor," he promised.

She giggled. "You're supposed to hold up three fingers, not two."

"No, this is right. I never made it past the cub scouts."

She burst out laughing.

With his two finger salute he vowed, "I swear on my slightly tarnished honor that I will try my best to keep my hands away from any of your good parts tonight...or *bad* parts, rather, since every part of you is pretty spectacular."

Shaking her head, she stated simply, "You're incorrigible." Releasing her hair from its ponytail, she added, "And unlucky for you, *so am I.*"

With just that one warning, his beautiful Abby proceeded to remove every stitch of clothing she was wearing, before sliding into bed next to him.

He gave a heartfelt groan. "You're a mean, mean lady."

"Goodnight, pup."

He loved hearing the humor back in her voice.

She turned over and parked her curvy backside up against his front side. But not in a lewd manner.

Shame.

He reached out and pulled her back into him fully, making sure he kept his hand on her belly—no higher or lower—as he snuggled her in. She stilled for a second and then relaxed against him.

"Good night, Abby."

"'Night Connor," she sighed in a voice already half asleep. "I missed you tonight, too."

The smile on his face stayed put, long after he began drifting off to sleep as well.

CHAPTER FOURTEEN

"YOU REALLY WANT to read my dissertation?" Abby was floored by Connor's request.

"Only if you're comfortable with that. I look over legal briefs and book-length contracts every day. You never know, I could help you see if there are any holes in your argument, or maybe find ways you could improve your write-up."

Who could pass up an offer like that? She grabbed the latest draft and held it out. Then yanked it back again. "Wait. You're busy with that huge cyber-company case. You can't possibly have the time."

"Actually, there isn't anything more I can do on that deal right now. Their decision on our latest proposal should be coming through either today or tomorrow." He snatched the folder out of her hands. "I'll read this while I'm eating lunch today."

Did he realize how many pages it was? "It's a few hundred pages."

He shrugged and downed the last of his morning coffee. "I took speed reading seminars during law school." Flipping through the pages, he estimated, "This should probably only take me an hour, if that. We can discuss it over dinner tonight."

That sounded so domestic, Abby warmed at the thought...before sobering back up an instant later. Heck, there'd be a Connor shaped hole in the door if he knew she was thinking of him in the happily-ever-after sense.

Which is precisely what she kept reminding herself when he leaned down to give her a quick kiss goodbye in a very have-a-good-day-dear sort of way. It was also what possessed her to purposely turn the heat up a nondomestic bit by playfully slipping her tongue past his lips. Then right back out.

The response was almost disproportionate.

His arms came barreling down around her, caging her against the breakfast bar as his tongue returned the favor in spades via a search and destroy mission for any and all non-sex-related thoughts in her brain.

Mission quickly accomplished.

"Don't start something if you're not going to follow through, sweetheart," he warned, dragging his lips over the side of her throat. "Because it's been nearly thirty-one hours since I've had you last. I'll damn well reassign every one of my court hearings today for a chance to be inside you right now. In a heartbeat."

How did this turn around on her so drastically?

With his forearms just barely touching either side of her ribs, and his warm, freshly shaven jaw under her lips, she was supremely tempted to strip him bare and have her wicked way with him.

But the shrill appointment reminder alarm from her phone tossed that possibility out the window.

"I-I have to meet with my committee advisor today," she replied, the raspy, untamed embers in her voice sounding practically 1-900-ish to her own ears. "Rain check?"

He nudged his hard arousal against the inside of her thighs, close, but not quite high enough to break her resolve. "You're going to owe me..." And then he did nudge higher. "...with interest." A kiss and a nibble, and then a soft, "Have a good meeting today," in her ear was his politely monogrammed acceptance of said rain check before he stepped back to straighten his suit.

She almost fell off the stool.

Now what meeting was she going to again?

———— ◆ ————

PULLING UP TO HER driveway, Abby couldn't believe how tiny her cottage looked now, after just over a week staying at the mini McMansion. Careful not to step on any industrial power cords or knock over any ladders, she slipped around back to where the builders were making excellent progress on the patio enclosure. "Hey Tom," she called out to the foreman.

"Abby, hi." A worried look flashed over his expression. "We're not behind schedule are we? I could've sworn you were coming back next—"

"No, no. Don't worry. I'm just here to pick up some books I left behind."

Connor would collapse in laughter over that one, she thought to herself.

Tom raised an eyebrow. "Tell me what kind of books make you smile like that and I'll go to the bookstore right now and get a set for my wife."

She blushed. "They're just research books my advisor wants me to re-read."

"If you're looking for more *hands-on* research, honey, count me in," called out the journeyman passing by carrying sheets of drywall.

Goodness, her face would never return to its normal color at this rate.

Slinging a dusty arm around her shoulders, Tom led her away from all the whistling and howling echoing from his crew. "You're too easy to tease."

She walked with him into the kitchen and offered him a bottled water, taking one to cool off her cheeks. "You guys are horrible," she pouted, chuckling despite herself.

"Hey, I meant to ask, are you staying over at Connor Sullivan's place?"

Abby looked over at him warily.

"Don't worry, I'm not following you or anything. It's just I pass his home on my way over here and I could've sworn I saw your car parked in his driveway—the duct tape on the bumper is pretty distinctive."

Oh. The tension quickly left her shoulders. "He's my best friend's brother. When he heard I needed a place to stay for a few weeks, he offered me one of his guestrooms."

Tom nodded. "Yeah, sounds like him. He's a really great guy."

Surprised at the familiar tone, she asked nosily, "How do you know him?"

"He helped me and my brother out big time when we thought our business was done for."

That didn't make any sense. To her knowledge, Connor only did legal work for huge corporations—small construction businesses like Tom's weren't his normal clientele base.

At her puzzled expression, Tom explained, "It must've been five, six years ago, I think. Back when we'd just started the business. We'd been up and running for two years, making a decent name for ourselves by word of mouth referrals all over. The money was good, but not great. Mostly since there were long pockets of down time between projects. And that's exactly why, after one really slow month, my brother decided he wanted us to take a shot at flipping houses. You know, like they do on TV? I wasn't so sure about the whole thing, but he'd made it sound so easy, especially since we'd be doing all the work ourselves. So, I eventually got on board."

"And at first, he had been right. We flipped five houses in half a year, and made twenty times more money than we would've made just picking up reno jobs here and there." He shook his head in a big brotherly way. "But then my brilliant brother wanted to go after a bigger fish—a foreclosed mansion in Scottsdale."

Tom nodded when she winced. "Yup. It was waaay too big a fish. We had to start taking money out of all our accounts just to cover the expenses; the house was just so frickin' huge. The finish fixtures alone bled us dry since up until then, we hadn't gotten all those high end fixtures. But our real estate person told us that if we went with the more standard stuff, the house just wouldn't sell. Not in this neighborhood. So, we cleared out all our savings to cover it because at that point, we couldn't even afford to stop."

Abby couldn't believe how angry he suddenly looked. Since meeting him a few months ago, she'd never once even seen the guy frown. He was just the jolliest man.

But at this moment, he looked downright scary.

"We worked nonstop to get the house ready as quickly as we could. Then fate threw us the worse possible curveball. With just a few days of work left before we could officially sign-off on everything and list the house for sale, a bunch of kids broke in and partied it up in there. Jacked the whole house up in the process, from top to bottom."

Jesus. Now, she was scowling right along with him.

"We went in the next day to broken glass, graffiti, doors hanging off hinges, gouges in the hardwood floors, vomit and other crap all over the new carpet...shit, the place was a mess. These kids were frickin' insane. The banister was hanging off the stairs with some rope strung from it like a noose, some of our tools had been launched up at the ceiling, and they'd even bashed something straight through one of the main weight bearing walls."

He put his elbows on his knees and took a few calming breaths. "Anyway, I guess some neighbors finally called the cops and the kids all ran so they didn't even catch who did it. The damages were in the hundreds of thousands. And our insurance would only cover part of it, in chunks, paid out over weeks if not months down the line. At that point, we knew we were through. We were shitting bricks over the house staying on the market past a few weeks even before all the vandalism. There was no avenue left for us to take; the general consensus with our financial advisors was that both my brother and I would have no choice but to declare bankruptcy both professionally, and personally."

Abby could hardly breathe. It didn't take a genius to figure out the rest, but she still wanted to hear the words, hear someone else speak about Connor the way she and Brian saw him.

"Just so happened Connor was driving by that day. I guess he'd been at a client's house or something nearby. After seeing me and my brother talking to some cops and then some suits from the insurance company, he pulled over to ask what happened. He mentioned he was a lawyer and I thought he was just an ambulance chaser at first. But then we got to talking. Long story short, he ended up buying the house as is at a more than fair price. Then after the sale went through, he hired us back on to make all the fixes."

Well, that solves the mystery of why Connor lives in such an extravagant house.

"Connor totally saved our asses. And to top it off, he referred us to a bunch of new, very rich clients. By the time we finished his house, we were booked a year out for jobs all over Scottsdale and Paradise Valley." A long, emotional breath shot out of him. "My brother and I owe him everything."

At some point, Abby had stopped being able to focus on what Tom was saying. She could barely hear him over the deafening sound of her own heartbeat echoing in her ears.

It was just a story, why was she reacting so strongly to it?

Stupid question.

Saint Connor saves another one.

First his brother and then perfect strangers he met driving past a vandalized house. The man was so...so *frustrating*. That whole bad boy part of him was just one tiny, inconsequential part of him that he so wrongfully defined himself by.

Inside that hard, gruff exterior was a kind, caring man. A sweet man. A man that seemed to be hellbent on buying up every ripe avocado in the area to make sure she'd have an endless supply of guacamole while she was staying at his home. Simply because she'd mentioned that was her dissertation writing snack of choice.

Out of nowhere, she saw Tom waving a hand in front of her face.

She blinked and focused back on him again. Shoot, had he asked her a question? If he had, he didn't repeat it.

Instead, he just teased, "There's that smile again, Abby."

CHAPTER FIFTEEN

CONNOR WALKED into his office, closed the door, and sat down before he let himself go quietly ape shit.

$7.3 billion.

That was the unexpectedly sudden, final closing agreement for the complex multi-corporation dual merger and acquisition case he'd devoted the last five months of his life to. Seven-point-three *billion* dollars.

Taking a deep breath, he stared out the window at the picturesque view that his equity partnership had bought him in the firm, even though he was way too keyed up and pumped full of adrenaline to see anything really.

Seven-point-three.

Billion.

Absently, he reached over and flicked the little stress

reducing toy Abby had given him last week—a colorful little monster with wobbly arms, crazy troll hair, and a suction base that kept it secured to his desk for even the strongest stress-flicks to its googly-eyed head.

Talk about sticking out like a sore thumb. It didn't go at all with his office décor and yet he found himself keeping it front and center next to his phone on his executive mahogany desk.

Because it was weird and funny in the cutest possible way, just like Abby.

And that's why he loved it.

No woman he'd dated in the past would've gotten him anything like it. Nor would any of 'em have gone to the trouble of looking up the 1971 Charger to learn all there was to know about the car's history. But Abby had. In fact, she now knew more about his car's engine stats than he did, something she'd excitedly displayed all throughout breakfast this morning.

It'd been adorable.

Then she'd gone and done the exact opposite of adorable by slipping him the tongue in what was supposed to be an innocent goodbye kiss. And he'd experienced an actual leave of his senses. He'd been ready to throw her up against the nearest table, floor, or wall and have all kinds of circus sex with her.

It was a near thing, too.

If the appointment alarm on her phone hadn't sounded, there was a good chance he'd still be there right now going for round two…or twenty.

He flicked the stress monster again.

Before he fully realized he was doing it, his fingers were reaching for his phone and dialing her number.

"Hello?"

"Hey." Okay, now what? Another flick. "So…we closed the deal for $7.3 billion today."

The sound of books falling on the other end of the phone line had him sitting up taller. And grinning. She'd dropped her books for him.

"*Oh my gosh*, congratulations! Was it the carve-outs you renegotiated that sold them? I bet it was. Oh, but what about all those re-management concerns you had for the merger side? Did the spin-off push anything back at all? I know you were worried about the intellectual property on the acquisition end." Somehow, all of that came out as one long sentence. But she wasn't done yet. "$7.3 billion?! Holy crap, Connor! Were all the parties happy with the new deal? What am I saying? Of course they were. How are you not completely freaking out right now?!"

Connor laughed silently when Abby finally dragged in a gasping breath. Christ, she was priceless. "When I get home, I'll be sure to give you the short version of everything that happened, sweetheart."

"Screw the short version, I want to hear it all. It's a good thing I made—"

Silence.

"Abby? Hello?"

"Sorry, yes, I'm still here."

He frowned. "Are you okay? You got cut off there for a bit."

"I dropped my phone."

That sounded like a lie. "Okay…well, what were you saying? You mentioned making something."

"Oh, it's nothing. I can save it for another night. I'm sure you have some big celebration planned with all your colleagues. So of course the short version, definitely. Even if I'm sleeping, come wake me up okay? I'm dying to know the details."

For crying out loud, he wanted to wrap her up in his arms and kiss her senseless. She actually thought he was going to celebrate without her tonight. "Abby, I've seen way more than enough of my colleagues for the past five months. I want to spend my night with you, share everything that happened today with you. If you don't want to cook whatever you had planned, we can go out. Anywhere you want."

"Anywhere *I* want?" Her voice still had that heart-tugging hesitancy. "We should go where ever *you* want to go."

That was a first. To his knowledge, the standard reply to that offer was usually the most expensive restaurant and/or the most exclusive club. At least in his experience with women.

He embraced the novelty. "Well, if you're going to let me choose, I'd kind of like to stay in."

"Really?" He could almost see her skeptical frown through the phone.

"Yes. But again, if you don't want to cook, I will. Or we can do take-out."

"You're being ridiculous. Of course I'll cook. This is your big night. But are you sure you don't want to—"

"I'm coming home for dinner, Abby. Period. I'll be there at eight." Damn, that sounded light years away. Maybe he could cancel his next few meetings…

"If you're absolutely—"

"*Abby.*" She was so freakin' precious.

"Okay, okay. Yes, eight o'clock. *But,* if you make it nine, you can probably get in some celebratory drinks with your friends and that'll give me extra time to make something way more elaborate and—"

"I'm hanging up now, sweetie," he sang out. "See you tonight."

All he caught after that were razor sharp snippets about pigheads and horse butt as he replaced the phone back in its cradle. Knowing Abby, she could've easily been talking about him or the menu she had planned.

Either way, this was already promising to be an interesting night.

———◆———

AT EIGHT O'CLOCK on the dot, he walked in his house to the sight of Abby bursting out from the kitchen at full speed. She launched herself at him and peppered his face with kisses. "Congrats, congrats, congrats!"

Chuckling, he caught her face in his hands and gave her a long, slow kiss.

"You smell good." He stopped and sniffed again. "In fact, this whole house smells good. What is that?" Definitely not pighead or horse's butt.

She gave him a strange look. "Cookies."

He looked over and sure enough there on the big granite island was a platter of freshly baked cookies. He grew still as a statue.

"What's wrong?"

He was wondering the same thing as well.

And then it hit him. "No one's ever made me cookies before."

In no way was he prepared to see tears wash over Abby's eyes. Though she covered it up well with a whole lot of blinking, he saw the pain there—pain for the boy whose mother had never made him cookies.

Pain for him.

"Well, that puts a bunch of pressure on me," she said, audibly modulating her voice. "Hopefully, you have the same taste in cookies as your niece."

Now that she mentioned it, he did recall Skylar raving about Abby's world famous cookies. "How long have you been baking these for her?"

She shrugged. "Since Beth's hands started failing her pretty early on, it was hard for her to do things in the kitchen so...I don't know, maybe kindergarten?"

He picked up a cookie and felt a strange desire to crystalize the moment, savor his first bite of a cookie made just for him.

As his teeth closed on the warm, chewy treat, he looked over and caught Abby gnawing on a thumbnail nervously, waiting for his reaction.

He wanted to crystalize that moment as well.

"They're delicious." His voice was rougher, thicker than usual.

She averted her eyes again. "Oh, good. I'm glad you like them. I didn't know how else to help you celebrate your big win. I tend to defer to baking for all things celebratory...which is why I keep an extra pair of jeans the next size up when any holidays come rolling around..." She was babbling adorably, seemingly unable to stop. "I'm sure you're used to more lavish hooplas—"

He grabbed her and kissed her again.

As his male ego was pleased to note, that seemed to ground her. By the time he relinquished his hold on her lips, she was smiling again. "I made pot roast in the crockpot. Since you're such a fan of good ole fashioned dishes and all, I called my mom for her recipe and wrote it out on an index card for you so you can add it to your collection."

The gesture tugged at his chest. More and more, in unique little Abby ways, she was burrowing the most unlikely, but clear cut path to his heart.

He was going to miss her when she was gone.

It hit him then how different the house was going to be tomorrow after she left…after she went back to her *own home*. His gut clenched at the thought, rebelled against the notion of her calling anywhere else home since his only concept of the word for the past few weeks had existed around her.

Because of her.

And now he didn't want to give that up, didn't want her to go back to a home that he wasn't in, didn't want to think about the other inevitable reality he knew he'd have to face a few weeks after that.

The end of their month together.

Somewhere between his bedroom door and his closet, he was struck with the inane thought that there were thirty-one days in August.

One extra day in the month.

It stood to reason that his arrangement with Abby could be a thirty-one day month instead of thirty…never mind the fact that in the past few one-monthers he'd had, he'd been paring it down to four square weeks.

The lawyer in him told him it was a completely asinine argument to make, but some other unnamed voice inside him said it was genius, and that they were to present the discovery to her as soon as possible.

Because what it all boiled down to was the one thing he'd risk making a stupid argument for.

Another day with Abby.

"Okay, it's ready!"

Blinking himself back to the present, he quickly changed out of his suit and headed back down to rejoin Abby. Halfway there, however, he got sidetracked by a little piece of paper sticking out from her bag on the couch.

The first bolded sentence of the email printout caught his attention before he could stop himself. Then the second sentence had him outright invading her privacy.

He smiled, picked up the paper and brought it with him into the dining room.

"Why didn't you say anything?" he asked, coming up behind her and slipping his arms around her waist for a warm hug.

"About what?"

"About getting an article accepted for publication."

She spun around and snatched the printout from his hand.

Even though she was remaining impassive, he could see her eyes practically dancing the conga.

"I was going to tell you tomorrow. Since it's not exactly on par with a $7.3 billion dollar deal and all."

His eyebrows shot up in surprise. "Where's the woman who reamed my ass for downplaying her accomplishments just the other week?" he asked sternly. "You getting an article published in a journal is a very, very big deal. Completely on par with my news."

Her lips curved up at the corners.

"So we should celebrate," he suggested, nuzzling the side of her neck.

"We already are."

"But this is your gift to me. I want to give you something you want. So tell me. How can we celebrate your amazing news? Name it and it's yours."

She gnawed on her lower lip and then asked shyly, "Before or after dinner?" The way she was now rubbing her sweet backside against him was a pretty good indication of which she'd prefer.

He grew hard in an instant. *"Before."* Wow, he sounded almost primitive just then.

"Okay." She pushed him down into one of the dining chairs. "We'll do my celebration first and then we can have yours." Tugging on his button fly, she teased, "I hope you're not too hungry…because what I want isn't going to be all that quick."

That's what she thinks. With her curious hands all over him, he was ready to go off like a rocket ship at T-minus counting.

But then she moved those hands off his jeans, and placed them on top of his. At his questioning look, she smiled. "Keep your hands on the sides of the chair."

She couldn't be serious.

"I'm serious."

Damn.

"No touching." She slid up his shirt and trailed tiny tortuous kisses across his chest…down his stomach…

Jesus.

Eyes half-lidded with lust, she murmured softly, "What I want for my celebration is to have full reign over your body...starting *here.*"

Holy hell.

Her hot little mouth was going to have him 'celebrating' in about thirty seconds if he didn't get some control, fast. He steeled himself, gripped the edges of the cushion until his knuckles were strained white, almost painful.

But any marginal progress he'd made by that move was undone, however, when she kneaded her hands up his thighs and then along the base of his shaft, gripping him tight as she slid him deeper into her mouth.

His hips lifted sharply off the chair. Just once. He couldn't help it. She was driving him crazy. Crazier still when she purred in pleasure at the hard, quick thrust.

He let out a tortured groan, a wordless warning to her that he'd come soon if she didn't slow down or— heaven forbid—stop.

Another thrust, another purr and she was locking her eyes on his, holding his gaze as she slowly, slowly took him all the way to the back of her throat.

Fireworks exploded behind his eyelids.

He forgot all about her rule then and reached out to spear his hands through her hair, gently pulling her to her feet so he could pick her up and push her up against the wall.

His mouth crashed onto hers as he yanked a condom out of the pocket of his jeans and got it on in record time.

Pulling aside her panties, he poised himself at her entrance.

"Open your eyes, sweetheart. Let me see you."

When she did, he plunged into her heat.

Nothing, absolutely nothing had ever felt so good, so perfect. So his.

For eighteen more days.

CHAPTER SIXTEEN

———

"Why don't you stay? The construction guys are still going to be coming in and out of your cottage, finishing up. It'll be hell on your concentration," reasoned Connor as he kept an unyielding hold on her last fully packed suitcase.

And for the umpteenth time that morning, Abby *almost* gave in.

But she didn't.

Because the truth of the matter was that she wouldn't be able to bear it when he carried her luggage into the guestroom instead of his own room.

Her firm headshake wasn't enough to dissuade him, however. "C'mon, you have way more room here to spread out your research. Plus, you have a gourmet kitchen to help you tour the world in style, not to mention a very efficient dishwasher that'll work for kisses and heavy petting."

Abby chuckled and pasted an overbright smile on her face. "Tempting, but it'll be better for me to be back home before school starts."

It wasn't lost on her that the word 'home' tasted weird and chalky in her mouth now...all because she and Connor would no longer be using the word to refer to the same place.

Yeah, it was definitely time for her to go.

She hugged him tightly. "I had such a great time, Connor. Thank you so much for letting me stay here."

Why did that feel like goodbye?

He held onto her hand. "Have dinner with me tonight?"

She couldn't. She couldn't keep playing house with him. Couldn't keep finding new and better reasons to fall for him even more, to lose even more of her heart to him. She had to be strong. Protect herself.

"Can we do it tomorrow night instead?"

Oh yeah, real strong, Abby.

His hand tightened around hers for a bit, and then slowly let go. "Of course. Tomorrow night it is."

Remember, you can't keep him. You have to give him up in two weeks. At least that reminder had the desired effect. Steeling herself, she asked casually, "Did you want to go out for a change?"

It was a simple question and yet it was taking all she had to keep the tears from showing.

He stared at her silently for a moment before nodding. "Why don't we go to Le Mille Feuille?"

One of the most expensive restaurants in the area.

Her heart couldn't take much more. "Sounds great. I'll call you so we can plan a time." She quickly took her last suitcase from him and shoved it in her 'SUV'—even she was using the quotation marks now. She slammed the door. "I'll see you tomorrow then?"

"Tomorrow."

———◆———

ABBY FELT HER breathing go haywire when she heard the doorbell ring.

Aside from the one brief phone call they'd had to confirm what time he'd be picking her up tonight, they hadn't spoken at all since she'd moved back to her cottage.

Twenty-four hours.

She'd spent nearly that entire time at the library— reading, writing, arranging her books by cover color instead of topic. Anything in her power not to think about Connor.

Now here he was.

And all the work she'd put into walling up her heart was soon going to be tested.

"Hi, Connor."

Talk about failing with flying colors.

She was right back where she started weeks ago, losing herself in his intense blue gaze.

"You look gorgeous, Abby."

"Thanks. So do you." It occurred to her that in all their time together, they hadn't once gone out on a date.

Now she saw why.

They stood there awkwardly for a moment before he reached out and dragged her into his arms. "God, I've missed you."

The last bit of her ineffectual wall came crumbling down. "I'm sorry I moved our dinner to tonight," she blurted out then as she slid her arms around his waist.

He leaned back and brushed a thumb against her cheekbone. "Feeling bad about that are we?"

"Yes."

"Good." His lips came down on hers swiftly. The kiss was frantic, hungry. Just this side of angry.

By the time he pulled back, the room was spinning. "Don't ever shut me out like that again, Abby. Not unless you mean it."

No. She wouldn't push him away anymore. Couldn't. "Do you want to cancel our dinner reservations and eat here instead?" she asked softly, hopefully.

He slid his hand through her hair. "Actually, I'm kind of looking forward to having a night out with you."

"But—"

"Let's go out tonight, Abby. Let me prove to you

that we can do this."

How was it that he knew exactly what she was worried about? "You sound so sure."

"I am." He put his arm around her and tugged her over to the driveway.

To his beautiful powder black car.

With the bench seats she loved so much.

She smiled up at him. "Is your Lexus in the shop?"

He grinned back. "Nope. I told you, I'm going to prove to you that we can do this. You and I can be together and be ourselves out there in the big bad world."

"So you're going to a fancy establishment where you'll likely run into clients and colleagues?" *With me.* "In an old muscle car. Just to prove a point?"

"Abby, I'd pull up riding on the handlebars of Skylar's pink bicycle...hell, I'd drive up in *your car* to prove this particular point."

She burst out laughing.

"You don't believe me?" He reached for her purse. "Hand over the keys."

"No!" She giggled and ran the rest of the way to his car. "We can't go to a five-star restaurant in my car!"

Connor pinned her against the passenger door, capturing her lips in a deep, soul-searing kiss.

It wasn't until about five seconds after the kiss ended that she realized he'd gone and pickpocketed her purse.

A half hour later, Abby was still whacking him on the arm.

"That valet kid thought we were punking him." Another whack. "I swear, he kept looking around like a bunch of TV cameras were going to come rushing out."

"I know." He chuckled. "Did you see his expression when I slipped him a twenty and told him to make sure to park it somewhere safe?"

"Stop." *Whack.* "Making fun of." *Whack.* "My car!"

"Yes, *this* is far less embarrassing. Quick, sucker punch me in the gut. I think I see a lawyer from a competing law firm I'm facing in court on Monday."

She instantly dropped her hands back to her sides. "This isn't over," she hissed.

"Oh, I know. And I'm counting the minutes till we get home to see just what you'll do next."

Home.

She had no idea whose home he was referring to, but at least they'd be there together.

As the maître de led them to a corner table with a stunning view of the city, Abby couldn't help but sigh with pleasure. Not because they were in the most elegant restaurant she could ever imagine.

But because she was starting to believe.

"Thank you," she said quietly. "For proving your point."

Connor smiled back. "I think I'd much prefer a 'you were right.'"

She flicked open her menu. "I'll keep that in mind if one day you ever are."

His soft, tickled laughter died a quick death when a slick as silk voice rang out from the next table over.

"Why look Lynn, it's Connor."

They both turned to watch a tall, distinguished looking man stand up and come over with his 'date'— Abby would've guessed daughter at first but seeing his hand on the woman/girl's ass quickly dispelled that theory.

"Connor, did you get that paperwork I left on your desk today?"

So, a colleague, then. One that, from the looks of it, Connor didn't like very much.

"Yes, I did. I'll look over it in the morning," he answered brusquely, his eyes as hard and cold as she'd ever seen them.

The stranger didn't budge. "Well? Aren't you going to introduce me to your beautiful date, Connor?"

Abby watched a muscle tick in Connor's cheek as his entire posture turned rigid with anger.

Alarmed, and thoroughly lost, she stuck her hand out to the man to try and defuse the situation. "I'm Abby. It's a pleasure to meet you."

"I'm delighted to meet you, Abby. I'm Marcus, and this is Lynn my personal assistant."

Riiight.

"So, are you two here on a *date*?" inquired Marcus.

Abby could see why Connor didn't like him.

Connor's glare went from angry to furious.

"What?" asked Marcus innocently. "Can't I be just

a little curious about my son's love life?"

Son. The rude man was Connor's father.

"Lynn," Connor shot a withering glance at the woman fidgeting beside Marcus, "I hope you remembered to order my mother's anniversary flowers. You know how hard it is to get those lilies that she loves so much."

Lynn blanched and mumbled, "No, I forgot."

Marcus raised an eyebrow in a silent touché, before conceding, "Fine, keep your secrets, Connor. I guess I'll just have to get to know Abby better on my own." He turned to face her. "Perhaps at this weekend's charity ball?"

Abby froze, and did her best to keep her smile plastered to her face.

"That's enough!" barked Connor.

"People are starting to stare, Marcus," whispered Lynn.

Marcus gave Connor a triumphant look and then took a step back. "Well, I see the two lovebirds just want to be alone. Have a good evening. Sorry to have interrupted your *date.*"

Abby kept her eyes glued to the menu until he was gone. Really? Did he have to put such a scornful emphasis on the word 'date?'

"I'm sorry you got sucked into that." Connor's voice was literally vibrating with rage.

She dropped her menu. Connor shouldn't be apologizing for his socially corrupt father. "You have absolutely nothing to be sorry for."

He covered her hands with his. "That charity ball he mentioned—"

Oh. Well, there was that. "You don't need to explain."

"It's just an annual gala we all go to because the firm is one of the main sponsors. I forgot about it completely. Usually, I just take Victoria to these sort of things but if you want to go, I'd love to take you." He turned a shade uncomfortable. "It's a black tie affair. I, uh, could take you shopping for a gown. And I'd buy it for you, of course, since you're doing me the honor of being my date."

A little part of her died on the inside at the offer…and then rose from the dead out of sheer annoyance when she saw Marcus watching them with that same aggravating smile.

This was a vicious, vicious world Connor lived in. Surviving here took a whole skillset she lacked entirely.

"What night is this ball?"

"Saturday."

"I actually have plans for that night," she lied, giving him a wan smile. "So I guess I won't get to have my *Pretty Woman* shopping moment with you."

His hand closed tighter around hers. "I'll stay home if you want."

She shook her head vigorously. "No, don't do that. You should go have a good time." Wanting desperately to get some air, she stood up abruptly and looked around for a restroom.

He caught her by the elbow. "Talk to me."

"There's nothing to say. I just can't go. But I really, truly want you to have fun. Charities are important." She patted his arm reassuringly. "And despite her kissing you and offering you a member massage in front of me, Victoria does seem kind of nice."

"You're not upset?"

"No," she replied with complete honesty. "Just uncomfortable. Give me a few minutes to collect myself and I'll be fine."

"I'll give you five." He gazed at her worriedly. "If you're not back by then, I'm coming after you and we'll leave. We can go to that little Chinese restaurant you love so much." A genuine smile lit his face then.

Alright, *now* she was upset. But not at him. At his world. At his father. At everything that kept Connor tethered to the toxic things that were poisoning his life.

She rushed off to the restroom, knowing Connor would make good on his offer to whisk her out of there if she showed him even a hint of the anger she was feeling. But she didn't want to give his father the satisfaction. Even now, from where he sat across the room, Marcus Sullivan was visibly laughing at her discomfort in the most mocking, condescending way possible.

How a man like that managed to father two of the best men she'd ever known was a complete paradox.

Pulling open the ornate door to what was the most extravagant restroom she'd ever seen, Abby flipped on the water at the marble sink and stuck her wrists under the cold stream. Slowly, eventually, she felt some of her tension wash down the drain. She could do this. She wasn't going to let Marcus win. She was going to go out there with her head high and have a great night.

And if she accidentally keyed his car enroute to her own, oh well.

She smiled wryly at her reflection, knowing she'd never in a million years ever do anything like that.

"You're way too nice," she accused her reflection.

Before her reflection had a chance to reply, the sound of small commotion outside had her scrambling to the door. Had her five minutes lapsed already?

"*HEY!*" she yelled, when she opened the door and saw that the racket out in the hall had nothing to do Connor at all, but rather, a very large man shoving around a very small woman.

The second she saw the man start to rear back his arm, Abby set off on a dead sprint.

"*Leave her alone!*" She rammed herself right into the man's side, effectively budging him about two inches. He was a big man.

"What the hell?" The man swayed on his feet and glared at Abby. "Who the hell are you?"

She ignored him but kept one eye trained his way as she checked on the woman—good lord, she was tiny. The man could've snapped her like a twig. "Are you okay?"

The woman spewed out a long hysterical sentence.

In a foreign language.

Okay, that helped Abby not at all.

Sausage like fingers clamped onto her arm. "Hey, *nosy bitch.*" He spun her around like a top and Abby went flying against the wall. "Mind your own f—"

The loud crack of a fist connecting with his face stopped that f-bomb from landing.

Connor.

The man went down. But Connor wasn't done. He laid in two more punches before Abby realized he was planning on beating the man to a pulp.

"*Connor! Stop!*"

He didn't. And then all hell broke loose.

Two managerial types and a security guard came charging past to yank Connor off the man. Marcus swept in soon after spouting some legal jargon to a stricken restaurant employee while his 'personal assistant' started anxiously talking on two cell phones at the same time.

Nearby, the tiny woman was still screeching something in her own language and throwing her sleek stiletto heels at the sausage-fingered asshole, who'd begun puking all over his designer suit. And throughout it all, Abby saw that half the patrons in the dining area were still eating and carrying on like it was beneath them to even bother to look their way.

Abby shook her head. She so did *not* belong in this world.

Chapter Seventeen

CONNOR HAD NEVER BEEN more terrified in his entire life.

When he saw that drunken man throw Abby like a ragdoll, Connor had just plain lost it.

Even now, he could barely piece together what had happened immediately after. If not for the half-dozen or so witnesses who'd managed to fill in his rage-filled blanks for the police report, there was a good chance he would've been arrested for lack of cooperation during the follow-up interrogation alone. Because honestly, he'd been unable to answer most of the police questions definitively, save one: Abby had bum-rushed a man easily twice her size to protect a woman she didn't even know.

Who does that? Who is *that* good of a person?

Abby.

After he'd taken her home, he'd simply held her the entire night, not sleeping a wink. Over and over in his head, he replayed the sight of Abby being slammed into that wall, imagined what would've happened had he not gotten there in time.

It could've been so much worse.

As it was, Abby was sporting a bruise covering half her arm, outlined in the shape of each of the sonofabitch's fingers.

Connor fisted his hands in reflex and winced—his right fist was scabbed ragged all across the knuckles, while the left was the one that was still swollen and bruised.

A charming look with his tuxedo.

Flexing his fingers to ease the ache, he looked around the ballroom, still in disbelief that Abby had convinced him to attend the charity ball. He hadn't wanted to leave her side all week; tonight was no exception. But she'd reminded him about her prior commitments for the evening and urged him to go.

So far, he was having a lousy time.

And reason number one was sitting right beside him.

"Poor baby, do you want me to ask the waiters to bring some ice for your hands?"

He rolled his eyes. Had Gabriella's voice always been this annoying?

"No thanks, I'm fine."

He couldn't for the life of him remember why he'd

slept with her, let alone dated her for an entire month. She was fake, vapid, and dull as dirt.

The anti-Abby.

"Do you want me to kiss it and make it all better?"

Ugh. Baby talk? Really? "I'm going to go get a drink."

He stalked off, glad that she finally caught the hint and chose not to follow.

Seeing Victoria at the other end of the bar, he beelined it over and cornered her with a scowl. "I can't believe you abandoned me tonight."

"Can you blame me?" She pointed out her date, aka the manchild at her table who probably modeled underwear for a living. "That is one fine specimen of a man."

"The guy's half your age, Victoria."

"I *know*." She beamed. "Thank Marcus again for me, will you?"

Wait, what? He grabbed her elbow. "My father arranged this date of yours?"

Her brows snapped together. "He told me you were fine with it."

At Connor's exasperated sigh, she thunked her drink on the counter. "Oh shit, you didn't know, did you? I *thought* it was weird you and Gabriella both showed up dateless." Now she looked genuinely apologetic. "Connor, you know I'd never knowingly play a part in one of your father's schemes, right?"

No, Victoria was many things, but a backstabber of the people she cared about wasn't one of them. "Don't sweat it. My father's up to something. There's no way you could've known."

"Still. I can't believe that asshole used me. *Me.*" Victoria's eyes narrowed on the asshole in question at the other end of the room.

Connor smiled. If he weren't already planning his own confrontation with the man, he'd be more than happy to sic Victoria on him. That was one woman you did not want to mess with.

He took his drink over and sat down in the empty seat beside his father, shoving Lynn's personal assistant necessities—aka the purse with all the condoms and the little blue pills—to the side. "Why are you trying to surgically attach Gabriella to me?"

Marcus nodded approvingly like a—gag—proud father. "She's a lovely woman isn't she?"

"Cut the crap. I asked you a question."

"I'm doing you a favor, Connor. Embrace it. Gabriella is much more suited for you than that...girl you were with the other night." He shot a reproachful glance at Connor's injured fists.

Connor officially lost what little patience he had at that point. "I'm going to ask you one more time. What the hell are you up to? You tell me this instant or I'm going right over to Gabriella to cause a scene that will make the fight at the restaurant last week look like a frickin' party."

Ice cold irritation flitted across his father's face. "Well, if you must know, the announcement hasn't been made yet but I'm going to be retiring at the end of this month."

"Congratulations. Now what's that got to do with me?"

"It's a forced retirement," he bit out through his teeth. "And it's all your mother's fault."

Connor stilled. "How is she a part of any of this?"

"The woman's lost her mind. First she kicks me out of my own house and files for divorce. Now, she's coming after my throat, threatening to expose all the married women I've had affairs with if I don't give her everything she wants in the settlement." He gave a disbelieving grunt, but Connor could hear the film of fear behind it.

"What are we talking here? Clients? Judges? Politicians?"

It had to be one or all of the above for the firm to be forcing him to retire.

"It doesn't matter. I have all our best lawyers on it. Thankfully, your mother's legal counsel is subpar at best. We're handling it."

God, he really was a bastard. "Why don't you just give her what she wants? Lord knows she deserves it. You've been cheating on her and treating her like shit for over half her life."

"What the hell do you know about any of it?!"

"I know enough," replied Connor coolly.

"You just think you do. Because you're still behaving like a fanciful child. We had a marriage arrangement, clear and simple. She's being unreasonable. Perhaps you could talk some sense into her."

Over his cold dead body. "Look, you've now wasted ten minutes of my time. Either tell me what you and Gabriella are up to or I'm going to go grab the mic and entertain the room with all the kinky shit she's into."

"This is all because of that college girl, isn't it?" hissed Marcus.

"You dare say one negative thing about her, and this conversation is through."

"I'm just looking out for your best interests!"

Since *when*?

"Connor, you have a chance to be name partner."

"What the hell are you talking about?"

"I've been talking with Timothy Knight from Knight and Stern."

"As in Gabriella's father?"

"Yes. Her father is interested in my partnering in their firm."

"Why on earth would they want you? You'll be damaged goods once the divorce proceedings start."

"Regardless, I have the deep pocket clients they want."

"None of whom you'll be able to take."

"Yes, but *you* can. After my 'retirement.'"

"Whoa, whoa. I'm not jumping ship. And even if I

wanted to, I sure as hell wouldn't jump into a new one with *you*."

"Not even for a name partnership? I've worked it all out. By the time I'm through, Sullivan, Knight, and Stern will be—"

"Just stop! I'm not taking part in this scheme. If you're going to join Knight and Stern, it's going to be without me. And if my personal life was somehow part of this deal you're negotiating with Timothy Knight, you better start thinking of a back-up plan because not only am I not leaving the firm, I'm not going to come within ten feet of his daughter."

"Because you're in *love*?" sneered Marcus.

Connor remained silent.

"I knew it," he spat out with contempt. "You're chasing a girl who's too nice to admit that she's been in love with your brother for over a decade. Don't you have any pride?"

Connor felt that blow clear to his gut.

"What's more, your brother is in love with her too. He just hasn't realized it yet because of everything that happened with Beth. But he will. And when he does, do you really want to be the one standing in his way?"

Marcus did an almost believable impression of a fatherly sigh. "Your brother is a good man. He stood by his wife through an awful disease and is now raising his daughter as a widower. He and Abby are perfect for each other. They're both family oriented, both educators. If you really believe you're falling for this girl, stop thinking with your dick for once and do the humane thing. Nip this in the bud. She'd never survive in your world and you know it. She's a nice girl. Let her be happy with your brother. You'll never be able to give her the life she deserves, not the way Brian can."

Connor tried to get up and walk away, tried to stop listening, but he couldn't.

Aside from the farce of fatherly concern for Brian, nothing his father said was untrue.

Not the least of which were his feelings for Abby.

CHAPTER EIGHTEEN

———— ⁓⁓ ————

AT THE SOUND of the doorbell, Abby checked the clock. 9:30 p.m. There were only two people who could be standing outside of her house at this hour. And since both were well aware of her addiction to ice cream, she brought the pint she'd been working on along with her as she went to open the door.

She really shouldn't have.

Because apparently, James freakin' Bond had taken over Connor's body.

And she was rocking one of Brian's old shirts and a messy half-ponytail/half-bun piled atop her head.

"Hi, beautiful."

Her knees buckled.

"So this was the pressing engagement you couldn't

break to go to the charity ball tonight?" he asked, eyebrow raised.

"Yup. Ice cream night is a big night for me."

He leaned over and intercepted the spoonful she'd just scooped up. "Green tea? Right, you're in Asia this week. Nice. So are you going to invite me in?"

"Oh, of course. Come in. Why aren't you at the gala?"

"Because you're here." He tried to pull her in for a kiss but she grimaced and took a step back.

"What's wrong?"

She frowned. "You smell like perfume. And before you say it, I know you didn't do anything, it's still..."

"Right. Like the kiss thing. Well, as was the case then, I was completely innocent tonight as well. Gabriella was all over me like a barnacle I couldn't shake."

"Gabriella? I thought your date was Victoria."

"It's a long story that involves my father." He stole another spoonful. "I don't want to talk about it. Can we just hang out tonight? Do you mind?"

"Of course not." She started clearing off all the research books on her couch.

"Actually, while you're doing that can I shower first? If you think this perfume is bothering you, try wearing it." He made a face.

"Extra towels are in the cabinet above the toilet and if you check the third shelf in the hall closet, you'll see a bunch of Brian's clothes. Take whatever you want."

Connor halted and looked back her way. "Does he do that a lot?"

"What?"

"Leave his clothes here?"

She shrugged. "It's a collection that's been building for years. It's mostly from the times he used to pick up Skylar after seeing Beth. He used to shower as soon as he got here to get the hospital feel off of himself."

"You wear a lot of his shirts."

She studied his hooded expression. "Because they're comfortable. Connor, are you okay? What happened tonight?"

"Still don't want to talk about it," he called out, pivoting back on track for the bathroom.

It was a good five minutes before Abby heard any signs of life that confirmed he'd made the journey successfully.

"Hey Abby, can you come here for a sec?"

Walking into the wide-open bathroom, she was greeted by a sight infinitely more decadent than her ice cream.

A wet, naked Connor sitting in her tub.

He grinned. "Remember our first phone call?"

She shivered at the reminder. "Yes."

"Come here."

As she took the four short steps to the tub, Connor stood up and sent sheets of hot water rippling down his body.

Holy swizzle sticks.

He reached over and peeled Brian's old shirt off of her. And then skimmed her bike shorts and panties down her legs, trailing kisses across every new inch of skin he uncovered. "I'll never get over how gorgeous you are."

Likewise.

She stepped into the tub and straddled his thighs, smoothing her hands all along the hard, muscular planes of his chest and abdomen…god, touching him was an art of foreplay all on its own.

Speaking of touching—

She gasped. "You went snooping through my drawers." In her head, the accusation was a whole lot more indignant. Way less breathy.

"No bath is complete without a few toys."

Good lord, why did this feel a thousand times better when he was doing it?

Feeling the sensations quickly start to build to a crest, she grabbed his hand.

"Too strong?" he asked worriedly.

"It's fine," she said, pulling the vibe out of his hands. "But it's not you." She slid forward, gliding her inner thighs slowly across his erection. "I want *you* to make me come…inside me when I come."

His pale blue eyes turned dark and turbulent. "*Condom.*"

Abby smiled. She liked it when he turned Neanderthal.

As she reached over to the drawer under the sink to grab one, he swatted her behind lightly. "I'm not sure I like the idea of you having a big box of condoms just lying around your house."

She ripped the foil packet open with her teeth. "I bought it the same day I bought my pairs of red and white panties."

His grin lit up the bathroom.

When he reached for the newly opened condom, she held it away from him. "I want to do it."

Slipping one hand down his body, she stroked him gently, fascinated with the feel of him under water. Getting thicker and harder. For her.

"*Abby. God.* Put it on me. Now."

Drifting in a lusty fog, she blinked. Put what on where now?

Then she remembered. Too late. He snatched the condom from her, slid it on, and yanked her atop his lap, all in one slick move.

Her fingernails dug into his shoulders as he lowered his mouth to her breasts, circling one sensitive nipple with his tongue before moving over to score the other with his teeth. Back and forth, he kept her on the edge, varying his attacks, all the while staring at her like a hungry predator beyond ready to devour her.

Clutching her to him as if he'd never let her go.

Just when she thought he meant to tease her to the point of insanity, he lifted her up by the hips and plunged her down onto him. She gave a silent scream as he began driving into her deeper and deeper, harder and faster.

All she could do was match him thrust for thrust and hold on for dear orgasm as she felt the first waves of pulsing hot pleasure come crashing down on her.

Wrapping both arms around her, encasing her in a whole body restraint, he thrust into her one, two, three more times, before following her into oblivion with a fierce, primitive shudder.

———◆———

EVEN DAYS LATER, Abby was still replaying that bath with Connor. In fact, that's exactly how he had lured her back over to his house last night.

Two words: jet tub. And she'd been sold.

"So, you're still insistent on the dancing tonight, huh?" Connor snuck up behind her and slipped his arms around her.

Abby leaned back against him and made sure her smile was as bright as possible. "Yep. I got a new dress and everything." Well, not *new*. But new to her. And so gorgeous—flouncy skirt, sleek bodice, and shimmery black all around. It was her last night with Connor, and she was determined to go out in style, to make one final shining, sparkling memory.

Big and bright enough to possibly, hopefully eclipse the pain.

Connor sighed. "Fine. I'll be back at seven for our date. And I meant it about you staying here to do your research all day today. Skylar's going to be at her friend's this afternoon so you don't have any good excuse not to."

"And in case you get hungry..." he added quietly, "I got you a few avocados. They're in the pantry." He came to a full stop at the door and gave her a long, lost look filled with emotions she couldn't face. Not now. Not without breaking.

Don't look at me like that. Don't make me think about what tomorrow is.

Thankfully, he read her closed look and left without another word.

Unable to help herself, as soon as she heard his car leave, she went straight to the kitchen pantry. And nearly cried when she saw the mesh bag filled with twenty or so avocados.

God, this was going to be the most depressing date in history if she didn't get a grip.

With the most calming breath she could muster, she went over to her laptop and research notes, making sure only to take out what she needed. She didn't want to accidentally leave something here that she'd have to come back for.

She didn't want to be *that* girl.

She worked nonstop for an hour...and wrote exactly one sentence. All the words on the page were gibberish, her mind a mess. By lunch, she gave up completely.

Wandering upstairs in search of a distraction, the sight of her new dress was the only thing that effectively held her attention. It was so pretty. She didn't have anything else like it in her closet.

With no rhyme or reason whatsoever, Abby stripped down then and slipped the dress on. God, it was stunning. Elegant. Staring at her reflection in the full-length mirror, she hardly recognized the woman looking back at her.

The woman that Connor would be leaving come morning without a goodbye.

Had it not been for the loud chime of the doorbell echoing throughout the house, there's no way Abby would have been able to hold in the tears another second.

She quickly ran to the front door with the cocktail dress still on, store tag swishing.

"Hi, can I help you?" she asked the pretty woman standing impatiently out on the porch.

The woman just rolled her eyes and made to move past her to get into the house.

Abby blocked her way and attempted to remain civil. "Look lady, I'm not sure what you're selling, but we're not interested in any in-home demonstrations today." Okay, so maybe not *civil*.

The stacked redhead scoffed and looked down her obviously manufactured nose at her. "Please, don't act like you live here. I just need to get my purse. I left it here the other night when Connor and I...well, you know."

Liar! Abby struggled to keep a lid on her temper.

She detested women like this. "I'll make sure to tell Connor you stopped by. He'll find a way to get it back to you if it is here." Yes, and hold your breath while you're waiting.

"So high and mighty," snarled the woman, crossing her arms over her artificially inflated fun bags. "Don't think I don't know all about you. You're the little teacher Connor is banging this month. The one he's finishing up with."

No. There was no way Connor could've talked about her to this horrible woman.

The woman laughed at her stricken expression. "Oh, don't worry. He'll finish out the month. You know him, always one to fulfill his obligations. Especially his 'needy projects.'" She perched one perfectly French-manicured hand on her hip. "And when he's done with you, he'll come back to me."

"You're dreaming." Connor would never break his rule in that way. Especially not for a woman like this.

"No, *you're* the one dreaming if you think Connor's going to make your little Cinderella fantasies come true. If you don't believe me, ask him about the marriage arrangement his father is ironing out with my father as we speak." She ran a condescending gaze up and down Abby's frame. "Connor needs a trophy wife. And clearly, you're the furthest thing from a prize for a man like him."

Tossing her hair over her shoulder, she stalked off to her Porsche. "In a way, I'm actually glad he's slumming it for his last fling. It'll make him that much more appreciative when he's finally with me. So thanks for that."

Abby stood there, frozen in place. Unable to get her feet to move. Once in her car, the woman slid the driver's side window down and yelled out, "By the way, nice dress. Though it looked way better on me before I donated it to the thrift store...probably because it actually fit me."

With that, she drove off the property and Abby had to grip the doorframe for support. She felt like vomiting. Never had anyone been so intentionally cruel to her before. The awful woman's words clung to her like a web of venom, numbed her, made breathing next to impossible.

"Abby? *Abby*, what's wrong!"

A dozen beautiful red roses scattered across the doorstep at her feet.

Blinking slowly, Abby realized Connor was standing there holding her up, helping her back in the house.

How long had she been standing out there?

———◆———

"ABBY, HONEY? Talk to me. What happened?" Connor was officially freaking out. He'd come home for lunch to surprise Abby with flowers when he saw her white as a ghost on the front porch looking ready to faint.

"Are you feeling sick? Do you need me to take you to the ER?"

Abby shook her head.

He exhaled in relief. "Did something happen today?"

Slowly, very slowly, the color returned to Abby's face, and became replaced by…fury?

"That horrible woman! How could you ever have been with someone that vile?"

Shit. This did not sound good.

She picked up the flowy skirt of her dress, looked at it sadly, and then proceeded to rip the stretchy dress up off her body. "How can you live like this, Connor? These people…" She flung the dress on the ground and stared at it.

He couldn't tell if she was still sad or just plain livid now. "Sweetheart, tell me what's going on. Did someone come by?"

She laughed bitterly. "Oh, just some woman who said you two had sex recently. I believe she referred to herself as your future wife."

What?! Once wasn't enough. "What?!" his mouth echoed his brain.

"Tall redhead in a Porsche? The one who called me the cheap, fat pity project keeping you warm for her, before your upcoming feature-page nuptials."

"That goddamn bitch!" he shouted. "That's Gabriella, the woman who was all over me at the charity ball." Rushing over to Abby, he swept her up in his arms. "I am so sorry she did that to you. You can't believe a single noxious thing she said. She's working with my father on some harebrained scheme." He rested his forehead against hers. "She hurt you to get to me. And I'm so sorry for that, baby. So, so sorry."

Abby sagged against him. "I keep telling you to stop apologizing for these people. They're the ones at fault, not you."

But I'm the one dragging you into all this.

He kissed both her eyelids gently, thankful she hadn't wasted any tears on a whack-job like Gabriella. But the lines of strain on her face worried him.

This is exactly what he'd been afraid of.

Abby didn't belong with him. She was too good. Too *nice*. His world would undoubtedly kill her spirit, break her down and scrape away everything that was so special about her.

His father was right.

Abby was far better off with a man like Brian.

CHAPTER NINETEEN

"ABBY, WE DON'T HAVE TO do this. We could've just stayed home," Connor repeated for the tenth time as he pulled into the parking lot of the club.

"No. We were looking forward to going dancing tonight. I don't want that über bitch from today to ruin this for us." She unbuckled her seatbelt, looking determined to stomp into that club and dance away their last night together.

Keep pretending that everything was okay.

Meanwhile, Connor just wanted to hold her, keep her for himself for just a little while longer. Not just to ease her hurt, but to ease his as well. To preserve the part of him that she brought out, celebrated. *Loved*.

Even if it was for just a few more hours.

Knowing there was no convincing her otherwise, however, and knowing she was doing this as much for him as she was herself, he got out of the car and went around to open her door.

She beat him to it though, and was waiting for him with a sweet, sexy kiss. He took it greedily, drew strength from it and sank into it at the same time. Deepened it into something not so sweet. And a whole lot more sexy.

Mid-kiss, he felt Abby slip something into the pocket of his pants.

What the—

He pinned her back up against the passenger door. "What the hell do you think you're doing?"

Abby looked stunned. Her fun, flirty smile faded completely and Connor mourned the loss. But he was too on edge now to shift it into reverse. "What are you trying to prove with this stunt?"

He yanked her panties out of his pocket and waved it at her furiously. "That you can be just like the other women I've slept with? Just another one-monther?" He slid his free hand up between her thighs, punishing them both. "Is this what you want? For me to treat you how I treated them?"

His fingers met her wet heat. God, how was he supposed to walk away from this tomorrow? From her?

The question was one he'd asked himself a hundred times over the past few weeks, but it wasn't until tonight that he finally had an answer. It had killed him to see how broken down she'd looked after her encounter with Gabriella. Abby deserved better. She deserved to be happy. To be herself.

And if that meant letting her go, he would do it...because he'd gone and done the once unimaginable.

He'd fallen head over heels in love.

With a woman he couldn't keep.

Emotions now in overdrive, he went from teasing her slick flesh to plunging his fingers into her core, torturing himself with the memory of how hard she'd come against his mouth last night, knowing that he'd never get the chance to taste her again.

Not after this.

When he felt the telltale pulsing of her inner walls, he pulled her hair back and clamped his mouth over the soft skin of her throat, marking her intentionally, wanting to have some small claim on her for however brief a time period. Something to stamp her as his.

Before he had to let her go.

———◆———

ABBY WAS HORRIFIED at how her body was letting, *begging* Connor to keep going.

Keep telling her goodbye.

Keep punishing himself for having to do it.

Untamed and ruthless, his hands seemed to be everywhere all at once, using the secrets he'd learned about all her pleasures against her. For her. To drive her higher and higher…

His lips found hers just in time.

Saved the world from knowing that she was screaming her release in the middle of a crowded club parking lot.

Afterward, after she felt him cradling her to him gently, she drifted for a while. In and out on that lusty, floating bubble between repletion and awareness…until the boisterous laughter of a bunch of college kids walking past their car brought her crashing down to reality.

"I want to go home," she whispered, unable to meet his eyes as she scrambled back inside the car. She shut herself off from him before he could say another word.

When he climbed into the driver's seat and turned her way, she stared out the window, silently begging him all over again. For a different kind of release. *Please, please. Just drive. Give me that much, Connor.*

Finally, he did.

She closed her eyes to keep him from talking to her, to keep the tears from flowing. Because she knew what that was back there. That was Connor preparing to close the door on one of his one-month flings.

Preparing to close the door on her.

Turning away from him completely, she pretended to lean against her hand so she could wipe the tears away without him seeing.

"Abby, don't cry. Please, sweetheart. I'm so sorry.

What I did just now was unforgiveable. I don't know what came over me. It's just... You were being so different, doing exactly the kind of thing Gabriella used to do. And I hated seeing you do that, be that. For me."

He gripped the steering wheel, pain streaking all through his voice. "But that's no excuse. I should've stopped. You confided in me about your need for control and I all but stripped that from you back there." He sounded so appalled, so disgusted with himself, that her heart went out to him.

What was left of it at least.

All at once, it became too much.

As they rolled to a stop outside of his house, she shoved open the door and just started running, fumbling for her keys as she raced for her car, the sound of his thudding footsteps following not far behind her.

His hand came slamming down on the door, preventing her quick getaway.

"Let me go, Connor. Please. I can't do this. Don't make me go through this."

He tipped her chin up, forcing her to look up at him, to see his tortured expression, to see his blue eyes as gray as they've ever been. "I never wanted to hurt you, Abby."

"Then let me go. Because staying here for any more of your goodbyes *is* going to hurt me." She dropped her head to his chest. "*You were right.* Are you happy? It is more humane to walk out like a thief in the night without saying goodbye. Because there is no way that could hurt any more than what I'm feeling right now."

Hands fisting against his shirt, she whispered in anguish, "It didn't have to be like this. You didn't have to start pushing me away. We could have had our one last beautiful night together and gone our separate ways. Didn't you believe I could do it?"

"*You* weren't the one I was worried about, sweetheart," he said quietly. His arms wrapped around her and pulled her in close. "Even knowing that tomorrow is going to be the hardest thing I'll ever have to do, even knowing that I was a total ass who doesn't deserve to spend another minute with you, even knowing that you make me want to be the man that'll do what's right and just let you go…I can't. Not yet. If all I get are these last few hours with you, I still want them. God help me but I do."

She couldn't keep hearing him torture himself like this, denying them both the fantasy of a painless goodbye.

"I want those last few hours with you too, Connor."

————◆————

AS HE KNOCKED on the door to his childhood home, it occurred to Connor that he didn't have the vaguest idea if he still had his old key to the house.

There was a good chance he hadn't even taken it with him when he'd moved away to college. An even better chance that he had taken it, and then thrown it out with the trash one day.

"*Connor*? To what do I owe pleasure this early in the morning?" A surprised Helen Sullivan pulled her front door open wide and flashed the bright, formal smile she reserved for only her welcome guests. Oh, and her sons.

Connor grimaced. "Can't you just say hi to me like a normal mother for a change?"

She flinched.

Scrubbing a tired hand over his face, he tilted his head in apology. "I'm sorry mother, I'm just—"

"Can I help you with something?"

Her now utterly detached tone almost stopped him. But for some reason, he still managed to force out a quiet, "Actually…yes."

That brought her gaze swinging back. "Really?" She looked so surprised that Connor racked his brain to try and recall the last time he'd asked her for something. Not a single memory came to mind.

"I want to know why you're getting a divorce."

Her face became a cold mask. "You're the last person I thought would wonder over that. You know as well as I do that your father is a cheating bastard. A heartless bastard even without the cheating part."

He studied the first signs of life he'd seen in his mother in a long while. "How long have you known?"

"Since the beginning." She shook her head bitterly. "Your father made certain that I knew from day one. He wanted me to know exactly who and what he was, who and what I had contracted my life to."

For the first time ever, Connor felt something other than pity for his mother.

He felt empathy.

For a woman who hadn't felt strong enough to leave a marriage that was anything but, despite every cruelty her husband threw her way.

"Did you know going in? He says you knew. That it was all a part of the agreement."

She twisted her fingers around her now bare ring finger. When had she taken her wedding band off? How long ago did she file for divorce? What kind of son is callous enough not to know these answers?

"I knew it was all business for him, yes, but I never knew it would be a life sentence of pain for me. One filled with loneliness, humiliation. *Apathy.*"

"You didn't have to be lonely," he said quietly. "You had me; you had Brian."

His mother reeled back as if he'd slapped her.

And in a way he had.

Because before this, they'd never spoken about her lack of a role in his and Brian's lives.

"It wasn't that easy!" she exclaimed, showing actual emotion for the first time in what felt like forever. "Yes, of course I wanted to be there for you and Brian, shower you both with the love your father never cared to give. You were both my perfect miracles, both so strong and good— everything I wasn't. But living with your father, getting through each day in this sham of a life...I couldn't survive it without turning off my emotions. All of them. Because I couldn't just pick and choose certain parts of my heart to reserve for you and Brian, and not risk the rest of it to get slaughtered and stripped away by your father."

She gripped his forearm almost desperately. "You remember, Connor. How he always used to make us feel like we weren't worth caring about? It was a reminder he doled out daily, in a hundred heartless different ways. Even more so for me than for you two. And that was to keep me tied to him, a shell of a woman, too empty and broken to leave him."

"So what's changed?" he asked gently.

He had to know. Needed to know what could cause such a drastic change in a woman who'd made the choice every day for over thirty years to remain in her own personal hell.

"I fell in love."

Connor blinked. *That* he had not been expecting.

Throughout his entire life, where his father had always been disparaging about love, his mother had seemed incapable of it, oblivious to it. And why wouldn't she be? With a man like his father emptying her heart and making sure it remained that way.

After a long, cleansing breath, his mother began describing him then—her friend, the man who helped heal everything her husband had broken. The man who was waiting for her, apparently had been waiting for years.

For her to be free.

With each word, Connor watched his mother change before his very eyes. She became filled with joy, with life. Things that had never been there before, things she should've had a chance to have.

"You *are* in love." It was a statement, a fact. Even *he* could see it.

"It suits you," he added simply, not knowing what else to say.

Helen's hands squeezed his forearm in a gentle, motherly gesture he hadn't thought she'd know to do. "It suits you, too."

His eyes shot up to hers.

She gave him a sad smile. "I know. It's hard, isn't it? I fought it, too. Most people think that falling in love, *being* in love is so easy. But that's because most people have had it, or do have it. That's what family is supposed to be for, right? Your never-ending source of love? But you and I, we *didn't* have it. How in the world your brother found it despite everything is beyond me."

Her breath hitched. "And I will never, ever forgive myself for the part I've played in adding to that void in both of your lives."

"Mother, you did the best you could."

"No. I didn't. I should've been stronger. I should've loved you and Brian enough for two parents. Like how your brother is doing with Skylar. But I just…couldn't."

A sardonic grin tipped her mouth at the corner. "I

tried explaining it to Henry once. I'd likened it to having a limb fall asleep on you. It's compressed, drained, unaware...until that blood comes rushing in again. An unwelcome relief, or a welcome pain—depends how you look at it. Depends how long that limb has been cut off from circulation."

With a shudder of remembrance, she whispered, "And it hurts, almost unbearably at first to feel all that coming back in, doesn't it?"

Yes.

She nodded as if he'd answered aloud. "But it doesn't stop there. Sure, your sleeping limb is all filled up and whole again, but it's still not back to 'normal.' You still have to use it, get the feeling back, make it respond. So you get more doses of pain as you do, along with confusion, frustration, and at times, feelings that it's not really worth it."

"That's what my heart went through; the pain process was long, and just as terrible as it was wonderful. It wasn't until recently that it ended completely." She put a hand on his cheek—yet another motherly gesture he committed to memory just in case it never came back again. "But your pain is still going on, isn't it?"

Yes. A thousand times, yes.

"Who is she? Do I know her?"

That was an easier question to answer aloud. "You do, actually. It's Abby. Abby Bartlett."

Helen frowned, "Brian's friend?"

He nodded.

Surprise and sympathy drifted over her features. "Oh, dear."

Wow, for a woman just learning how to love again, she seemed remarkably insightful about all that he was struggling with.

Something that resembled a smile of motherly approval lit her face. "She is a very nice girl."

He almost laughed then. "Yes, yes she is."

"So what are you going to do?"

Sighing, he shook his head. "I don't know. Any advice?"

She started chuckling delightedly at that—another first. "I am the last person to give you advice on anything dealing with love, Connor, and you know it."

"Try anyway." He had a feeling she'd be better at it than she thought.

After a long moment of consideration, she said, "I think…if you love her, you should let her love you back, help her love you back. Because let's face it, we all need help with that."

She bit her lip nervously. "Did that make any sense?"

He gave her a small grin. "That's good advice. Great advice, really. Thank you."

Her eyes widened, and then softened with emotion. The new laughlines forming there yet another marked change he was happy to see.

"Can I give *you* some advice now?" he ventured softly.

A startled, pleased look crossed her features. "Of course."

He gazed at her for a beat, then smiled. "Let me and Brian call you 'mom' from now on."

An instant rush of tears filled her eyes. "Do you think I deserve that?" she asked, her voice a hopeful whisper.

"I do. I think you deserve to let us love you. I think *we* deserve that, too."

And now the tears were rolling down her cheeks. "I'd like that. Very much."

He stood then and they proceeded to have the world's most awkward parent-child hug ever. He shrugged. "We'll get better at it."

She chuckled—each one starting to sound more natural on her. "I'll be sure to practice the hugging with Skylar."

"Yeah?"

"Yes. And if she'll let me, I'm thinking of asking her to call me 'grandma.'"

"Good. That suits you as well." He glanced at his watch, knowing that even the best advice had a window of time before its shelf life expired.

If he was going to follow through on the one his mother had provided, he needed to head out now. "I better get going."

But before he did, he turned to his mother and asked, "This man, Henry, the one you're in love with—is he a nice guy? Does he treat you well?"

Her smile was resplendent. "Yes. Very much so."

"I'm glad. You deserve it." He walked another few steps to his car and stopped again when another thought occurred to him, the ugliness of his father's smug taunts from the other night echoing in his head. "Hey, who's your legal counsel for the divorce? I want to be sure you have the best if they're going up against our firm."

"I actually just changed legal counsel since it was clear your father was going to pulverize the first one I'd retained." She beamed. "My new attorney actually approached me to offer her help. Just last week, in fact."

Really? That was unusual. "Is she any good? Because I'll vet her for you, get you a better lawyer if you need."

"Oh, she's good alright. And you won't need to vet her. You know her very well."

He thought about that for a second before a slow smile pulled at the corners of his mouth. "Victoria?"

"Mmm hmm."

Connor tipped his head back and laughed. Until his face hurt.

His father was going to get creamed.

CHAPTER TWENTY

————~~~————

ABBY STRETCHED and rolled over in bed, sliding a hand over to the space beside her in reflex.

To the feeling of cold sheets.

So he left.

The tears came even though she'd told herself there wouldn't be any this morning. Even though she'd told herself she had no regrets about giving her love to a man who hadn't been able to give her his in return.

But no amount of logic and enlightened self-awareness could stop the pain, stop her from remembering every last detail of her final few hours with Connor.

A memory infinitely more painful in its perfection in the light of morning.

When the sound of the doorbell splintered through

her house a moment later, she stilled, unable to move, unwilling to allow herself to get swept away by the fantasy that it would be Connor standing there on her doorstep on day thirty-two.

And yet wanting to, so much.

Holding her breath, she walked over and creaked the door open.

"Hey, sweetie. Can I come in?"

It wasn't Connor.

She opened the door wide and let Brian pick her up and squeeze her in his usual big, burly bear hug. Had it really been a month since she'd seen him last?

"Hey stranger," she choked back her disappointment over which brother's arms were holding her, comforting her. "Why didn't you and Skylar come over this past week when ASU started back up? Were the three weeks without me that effective a detox program to get me completely out of your systems?" she queried, her attempt at humor falling flat.

"No. Just the opposite, actually," he said quietly. "But we stayed away to...give you your space."

She blinked and felt her already wobbly smile completely crumble away. "Connor told you, didn't he? He sent you over here?"

"Yes."

She quickly disentangled himself from his hug, which was now cloaked with sympathy. "What did he say?"

"A lot," he evaded, and slid a thumb over the new tear sliding down her cheek. "Don't cry, sweetheart. It'll be okay."

So saying, he pulled out a small, gift-wrapped box from the cargo pocket of his jeans and handed it to her.

She melted. Brian was always so good to her, such a good friend. She didn't know what her life would be without him.

"Open it."

Slowly, carefully, she slid her fingers under the seams of the wrapping paper—seeing as how this was the first time he'd actually wrapped a present for her, she wanted to savor it. Maybe even keep the ribbon.

When she peered into the box and saw the beautiful antique picture frame inside, the perfect size for her nightstand, she shook her head in unsurprised amazement.

Brian always gave her the best gifts. The photo he'd put inside the frame was her current favorite, too. It was taken the day she'd gone with him and Skylar up to the lakes earlier this summer. "As always, you're a mind reader. I love this photo. I actually just lost the copy I keep in my wallet."

"I believe that *is* the copy you keep in your wallet."

"What?"

Instead of explaining further, he just handed her a slip of paper.

Okay. Connor was right, Brian did have a flair for the dramatic.

She flipped open the note...and felt her heart spin.

> *Abby,*
> *Get out your magic decoder ring.*
> *You'll need it for the gift, too.*
>   *--Connor*

She whipped her head back up. "The gift is from Connor?"

Brian nodded.

A dizzying surge of hope flooded through her veins, rushed straight over to her heart as she called back the memory of what he'd told her once, but replayed it now with its heart achingly wonderful new meaning: *If I leave a note, then it's like leaving the hope that this isn't really goodbye for good...if I send a gift, hell, that's the same as saying I'll be back someday so don't ever forget me.*

No, she wouldn't need a magic decoder ring to figure out the note or the gift—what he thought he was giving her by this ridiculously romantic, misguidedly selfless act.

She blew out an exasperated breath, unsure whether to swoon, or cry, or drive right over to his house and kick him in the shins.

"What's wrong?"

Startled, she looked up, forgetting Brian was there for a second. "Your brother. He's what's wrong. Or rather, he *is* wrong."

"About what?"

Holding the note in one hand and the photo in the other, she gestured in frustration. "About this. All of it. He's doing all this to try to be 'the good man' over something that isn't even what he's made it out to be. This right here." She stared at the photo. "He obviously thinks you and I are something that we're not, something he insists on believing is better for me than what he and I have." No wonder he'd been asking her so many questions about Brian lately. Gazing at the note again, she sighed, "He's clearly built up this whole idea about you and me in his head, and he's not going to come back until I convince him he's wrong."

Brian reached out and slid a warm hand over her cheek. "What if he's not wrong, Abby? What if it isn't all in his head?"

End of Book One

———

Abby's Journey Continues In Book Two:

FALLING FOR THE GOOD GUY

Available Now

———

ABOUT THE AUTHOR

New York Times & USA Today bestselling author Violet Duke is a former professor of English Education who is ecstatic to now be on the other side of the page writing wickedly fun contemporary romance novels. When she's not writing or feeding her book-a-day reading addiction, Violet enjoys tackling reno projects with her power tools, trying pretty much anything without reading the directions first, and cooking 'special edition' dishes that laugh in the face of recipes. She lives in Hawai'i with her two cute kids and similarly adorable husband.

Get alerts on new releases and sales by email:
http://www.violetduke.com/p/join-email-list.html

Visit me at:
http://www.violetduke.com

For epic giveaways and other fun:
http://www.facebook.com/VioletDukeBooks

20832649R00137

Made in the USA
Middletown, DE
09 June 2015